"I never asked for you to take us out of school."

"I thought you'd have a good week. Away from your homework. Some bonding time."

"Nat may have bonded, but he's twelve. He's like a puppy. You do things for him, he loves you."

James broke eye contact, something he did not often do during those conversations. "Why don't you eat your dinner?" James' tone was now different—noticeably cold and downcast. "The last thing I want is for your mother to hear I've starved you."

With that, James stood up and opened the door that led to the kitchen. Nat could be seen at the table, eating his dinner unattended.

"Use whatever metaphor you want," Duncan made sure to say. "It still won't replace him."

James hesitated as if he was about to say something. But he finally turned and shut the door behind him, this time leaving Duncan and the now-cold dinner beside him.

1974

DUNCAN MANAGED TO CATCH the fastball. It took a few go-arounds, so when he finally clutched it, his dad instinctively pounded one of his fists in the air. The other one held a beer bottle, some of which spilled down the side from the sudden jolt of excitement.

"That's it, Duncan!" He said. "I told you you'd get the hang of it."

The ball lay softly in Duncan's glove, cradled admirably by that young, twelve-year-old boy.

"All right, this one's going to be a little different," Dad said. "This one's gonna curve."

But before he could throw another one, a voice called out from the house.

"All right, boys!" She leaned against the frame of the back kitchen door, her hip keeping the screen propped open. "I said five more minutes. You know when I said that?"

"Mo-om!" Duncan whined.

"You know when? Twenty minutes ago."

"It's the weekend," Duncan told her, since she didn't seem to understand.

"It's a school night."

"We're not gonna do anything anyway. It's the last week. They just let us play games."

"Oh, really? I guess I'm wrong, then. No more need for school."

For some reason, Duncan almost believed her.

"Pat, Honey. When will you be at the church building tomorrow morning?"

"Six thirty," Dad said. "As always."

"Great. Why don't you take your son with you? He essentially told me with his own lips that he's done with fifth grade."

With that, she slipped back into the kitchen, allowing the screen door to slap against the frame.

The two looked at each other for a second. "I think she's just kidding," Dad said.

But then a figureless voice echoed back. "Don't test me!"

So that was it. No more balls flew through the air that evening. Dad drank what was left in his bottle, then slung his arm over Duncan's shoulder as they trodded toward the house. But just before they made their way inside, Dad stopped him.

"Hey, bud." He bent down to eye level and rubbed Duncan's shoulder, looking unhinged at him during the brief silence.

"I've been wanting to talk with you," Dad said. "Mom mentioned you and Zack had a fight. Would you like to talk about it?"

At first, Duncan didn't respond. Then, noticing his dad's unwavering stare, shook his head ever so slightly. Dad waited.

"He wouldn't even sit with me at lunch on Friday," Duncan said finally, his tone bitter. "I was all by myself."

"Are you saying you aren't friends anymore?"

"That's what *he* said," Duncan told him.

"That's what Zack said? Really. Why would he

say that?"

Tears began to line the bottom of Duncan's eyes, crystalizing Dad and the scene around him.

"Listen, Duncan. Zack? He'll come around."

"You don't understand," Duncan said. "He was serious."

"We all say things we don't mean. Sometimes, we say them so passionately that we can't tell the difference. And you'll find that Zack's words, though as passionately as they were said, don't ring true."

Dad noticed his son's face tightening with anger and the redness growing around his eyes, and added, "Duncan. I'm telling you. Don't burn him in the hell of your heart. Don't do it. Or you might find yourself in the hell of God's heart."

His hand gently rubbed the back of Duncan's neck, both of them looking at each other with an unspoken understanding.

A tear slowly slid down Duncan's cheek. Dad wiped it with his finger, his eyes warm with affection.

"Forgive him," he said. "Be reconciled. Not to mention, you'll feel better."

Duncan found his voice. "What if he doesn't want to be friends anymore?"

Dad sighed, and Duncan found himself drawn into his father's arms and held there, his hair combed by those long fingers.

1980

THE COLD, SHALLOW CURRENT passed over the rocks, winding its way along the wood. Despite its stark coolness, the air was warmer those days, and the forest began to saturate with various shades of green. These were the days Duncan found himself enticed in returning to the crick with its silent and aimless sounds.

Nat, on the other hand, seemed drawn to *him*. "You could have slowed down," he said as if Duncan intentionally left him far behind.

"I wasn't running," Duncan said.

Looking up from the water, he found his

brother sporting an identical gray tuxedo as himself. Nat ambled in his direction and eventually leaned on the small, old-stained bridge, just as he was doing.

"Look," Nat said as he peered down at the stubby fish swimming along the riverbed. "Look how free they are."

"They're not free," Duncan stated. "You see how they move together? To be free, you'd see a fish on its own. Swimming by itself."

"They seem to want to swim together," Nat said.

"Until a predator comes and scatters them."

Nat narrowed his eyes on Duncan in confusion.

"And when the fish try to regroup," Duncan continued, "a few are gone. Other fish who don't belong come in. Some try to swim together, but others understand it's time to part ways. It's better that way."

At first, Nat's eyes moved upward, his head tilting slightly as if trying to calculate his brother's words. Then, his eyes returned to Duncan again.

"You know Mom doesn't like us coming out

here," he said, changing the subject, apparently unable to sum up Duncan's words in his head.

"Well, you know I still do," Duncan said back. "You're out here, too."

"Trying to stop you."

Duncan's eyes slowly shifted from Nat onto a sea of unclear thoughts. The sound of a distant, childish scream crept in and died away quickly. When he found himself brought back, Nat wasn't simply looking at him anymore. He was staring.

"Are you okay, Duncan?" Nat asked, leaning in, noticing his glassy expression.

Duncan stepped off the wooden bridge to follow the worn path back to their house, yet Nat wouldn't let his eyes off him.

"I wasn't running," Duncan said once more, though unsure of himself at that point.

He never glanced back, but Duncan could hear footsteps trailing behind him all the way home.

WITHIN THE NEXT FEW HOURS, Mom and James stood shoulder-to-shoulder at the altar while the minister read from 1 Corinthians 13:

If I speak in the tongues of men and of angels, but have not love, I am a noisy gong or a clanging cymbal. And if I have prophetic powers, and understand all mysteries and all knowledge, and if I have all faith, so as to remove mountains, but have not love, I am nothing. If I give away all I have, and if I deliver up My body to be burned, but have not love, I gain nothing.

Mom, with her cream-colored gown, and James, with his muted gray tux, looked overjoyed at one another. But when Mom looked past him to see Duncan's face, she could gather he did not share in the same intense happiness.

Love is patient and kind; love does not envy or boast; it is not arrogant or rude. It does not insist on its own way; it is not irritable or resentful; it does not rejoice at wrongdoing, but rejoices with the truth. Love bears all things, believes all things, hopes all things, endures all things. Love never ends.

Even after they made their vows, exchanged rings, and scurried out of the church building with intense applause and lighthearted expressions, Duncan could not will change his own. Not even after the music began, the food was brought out, and Mom permitted him a glass of wine. At the end of it all, he was the one who scurried away from under the festive lights and into the darkness.

As for prophecies, they will pass away; as for tongues, they will cease; as for knowledge, it will pass away. For we know in part and we prophesy in part, but when the perfect comes, the partial will pass away. When I was a child, I spoke like a child, I thought like a child, I reasoned like a child. When I became a man, I gave up childish ways. For now we see in a mirror dimly, but then face to face. Now I know in part; then I shall know fully, even as I have been fully known.

Duncan hid himself for the remainder of the evening behind the drawn bedroom curtains, not wanting to give himself away to the reception that was being held just below the window. Nor did he want to discourage his mom, who certainly wanted him there.

He sat and prayed, prayed and thought, until the area around his eyes grew gradually scarlet in color, the eyes themselves glistening under the lamplight. A few suppressed chuffs permeated the silence.

"Why so glum?" a voice softly rose.

Duncan hastened to wipe his eyes, partially to hide his embarrassment and partially to defog his vision. He looked up to find his dad standing just outside the bedroom door. In Duncan's disbelief, nothing audible came out, but Dad knew he was attempting to invite him in, so he took a seat next to him on the bed. They sat shoulder-to-shoulder for quite a while before Dad spoke again.

"You're all right, I hope," he said.

Duncan nodded at first but then sat still—like desert air.

"Why are you here?" Duncan asked finally, turning to face him.

"For you, of course." He hesitated. "And for your mother."

"Has she seen you yet?"

"No."

"Does James know you're here?"

"I don't believe so."

"It doesn't bother you?"

"What do you mean?"

"I mean—why are you here?" Duncan asked again.

"For you," Dad replied with the same answer.

"I don't understand."

"Isn't that what you want?"

"You're at *Mom's* wedding. And *you're* not with her."

Dad's eyes drooped slightly as if weighed down by Duncan's statement.

"Where were you?"

"Duncan—

"Are you going to stay?" he said, his eyes narrowing considerably.

Dad gave a long and burdensome sigh. "I can't," he resigned.

"Then why are you here?" Duncan's tone was now dissonant.

"I just wanted to see you," Dad said.

"And then leave again?"

"Duncan."

"Tell me where you're going. I'll go with you."

"No, Duncan. Listen."

"I will go with you, Dad. Let me go with you. I'm your son."

"You're not just mine."

"I'm yours, too, though!"

At this, Duncan found himself shouting at his father. He could sense his own heart rate pounding louder and feel his face wetting. Although there were no mirrors around, Duncan was confident he had morphed into something unsightly.

Dad didn't respond—not with words. Instead, he placed his hand on Duncan's neck and rubbed it like he used to. His other hand gently wiped his cheeks until his tears were dried. And he looked at Duncan as he had when he was younger.

Duncan wondered when they would sit this way again, arms leaning against each other's, finding warmth in the other's company.

1974

THE TASK HIS FATHER ASKED him to assist with was thankfully at its end. Beside the sawhorse now lay a small hill of measured-out pieces of wood piled on the open grass between the tree line and the backside of the white-clad church building.

"I'm gonna unplug the extension cord," Dad said as he situated his safety glasses back onto his ball cap. "Go ahead and start taking the planks down to the crick."

"Can't we just take the car?" Duncan moaned.

"Through the woods?" Dad said.

"On the street," He told him, feeling the need

to clarify. "We hardly go through the woods to go to service."

"Well, it was your great uncle's desire that we make a bridge between the two. Even though he passed away three years ago, we might as well fulfill it."

"He wouldn't be able to use it, anyway."

"Duncan. He pastored this congregation for over thirty years. He let us live in his house for free when we had nowhere to go. He left us that house in his will. The least we can do to honor him is build this little wooden bridge."

"It wasn't for free," Duncan said. "He had you help him."

"And look at God's providence. I'm now in his place. Pastoring the congregation he used to shepherd. Living in his home. And, of course, finishing that bridge he longed to do himself. Now, if you want to walk to the church building going the long way, that's up to you. The rest of your family will be using the newly built bridge— after *you* help me build it."

Dad followed the unraveled extension cord back toward one of the side doors, then vanished behind the white wall.

Duncan scooped in his arms a small bundle of what looked to be firewood, accepting that he could only carry so much—it would take a great many trips. He marched through the woods toward the place where they would be assembled. As he descended the worn dirt path, he heard a pickup sputtering into the church parking lot. There was a rap of two pickup doors on metal and a boyish voice that was only too familiar.

"Duncan!" Yelled Zack, a ways off.

"He's at the crick," Duncan overheard his dad tell him.

Without sparing a second, Duncan charged over the trail, paying no mind to the thistles on the pathway. Though, his attempt seemed futile as the distant footsteps drew ever nearer. In a last-ditch effort, his arms unwrapped themselves from the planks—which clunked on one another as they hit the dirt—and swayed in quick succession to aid his speed.

Zack reached the water, finding no one, and panned the wood hoping to catch a glimpse of his friend.

"Duncan?" Zack called out.

Nothing.

"Duncan!"

Just then, Zack winced, his hand raising to cover the back of his neck. He bent down and picked up the acorn that had apparently hit him. Then, his eyes slowly scanned the canopy above.

"How in the world?" Zack whispered to himself as his eyes found Duncan.

"You weren't at school today," Zack said, noticing Duncan was choosing not to respond. "Come on, Duncan. Get down. Let's talk."

"What about?" Duncan retorted. "You seemed okay not to talk to me all weekend. Or on Friday."

"I know," Zack said, his voice slightly repressed. "I've been stupid."

When he realized Duncan was content to remain silent, he went on. "My dad needed to see your dad. It seemed pretty urgent, I guess. I think we have time to hang out…if you want to."

"You didn't want to—

"Oh, come on, already. Are we friends or not?"

"You said we weren't!" Duncan shouted.

Zack finally seemed to understand his frustration. Peering down at his worn shoes, then back up at Duncan, Zack extended his arm as if to lend a hand, although they were nearly twenty feet apart.

"What's that for?" Duncan said.

"Get down and shake it."

"What *for*—

"The handshake of brotherhood."

Duncan exhaled deeply.

"Come on," Zack said, this time more lightheartedly, interpreting that sigh to mean Duncan was about to give in.

And he did. Duncan's feet found their way on the sturdy branches beneath and eventually landed on the forest floor with a thud.

Zack kept his hand outstretched, waiting for his. As Duncan approached him, he spit into the palm of his own hand. "Brothers?"

A moment's pause suspended Zack's word.

"…Brothers," Duncan said wearily back in surrender, his spit joining Zack's as their hands collided.

1980

FIVE DINNER PLATES WERE AT THE TABLE, though only four were sitting there. One remained vacant even as Mom stood from her chair to serve everyone her usual home-cooked special.

The first several minutes after James prayed were subdued with scrapes and chewing, which continued in undertones as conversation eventually rose.

"So, you're packed?" Mom said to Duncan, making sure what was in her mouth was swallowed first.

He nodded.

"I wish you hadn't forced him to go to a college a state away," she continued, now turning to James. "Seriously."

"I didn't force him, Sarah," James said. "He chose to apply."

"I suspect you were the one who told him about it."

"So," James said quickly, "Duncan. We should be out the door by seven to make it well before dinner."

"What if he gets into the wrong crowd?" Mom said, apparently not finished talking with James.

"What are you wanting to do, then? Go there and bring him home? Sarah, the boy's an adult now. We should be grateful he's not going to school on the other end of the country."

"Well…if he so happens to get into the wrong crowd, you better be sure I'm driving six hours to bring him home."

"Mom," Duncan said.

"Well," she repeated, her eyes sparkling and red.

"Dad went there. Why can't I?" Duncan

added.

"Now, look what you've done," Mom said, directing her statement to James again.

"Nothing's going to happen to him," James said, trying to reassure her. "If he gets so much as a tattoo, I'll remove it myself."

"I want a tattoo!" Nat finally spoke up.

"No," Mom interjected. "No tattoos."

"But James has one," he said.

"James is an adult."

James glanced down near his shoulder. Two eyes were inked over an organ—the heart.

"This?" He said. "Like it? My own creation."

"You tattooed yourself?!" Nat exclaimed.

"No. But it was a concept I had in my head. This was many years ago. When I was in the military. Kinda weird looking, isn't it?"

Mom must have felt like she lost the conversation, because she brooded while finishing the last of her asparagus.

DUNCAN SPENT THE FADING HOURS in his room, ensuring everything was in order. He checked that every necessary article of clothing was stripped from its hook and folded in the large cardboard box with the rest of them. Before folding it closed, he placed his worn calfskin Bible on the very top.

James was standing under the doorframe as Duncan turned to move the box from the bed. One of James' arms leaned against the doorpost, the other hidden beneath his pocket.

"Have you been standing there the whole time?" Duncan said with slight annoyance.

"I was just about to knock," James said, stepping into the room without a welcome.

He sat down on the edge of Duncan's bed and watched him place the sizeable brown box next to the door with the others.

"Another talk?" Duncan said flatly.

"Why don't you sit down?" he said.

"I'm fine."

James examined him, trying to figure out how to proceed. "Duncan."

"I won't get into the wrong crowd, okay? That's not the plan, anyway."

"It's not about that."

Duncan paused, waiting for James to tell him

plainly what this was.

"You're older now, Duncan. Eighteen. Off to college. It's time, I think."

"…For what?" He said, not appreciating James' cryptic message.

James reached his hand, as if in slow motion, into his pocket. Out came an envelope, colored with age.

"I've been saving—

"Listen. James," Duncan stopped him. "You're right. I'm eighteen. I'm an adult. You've done plenty. I don't need your money."

"It's not money," he said.

"It doesn't matter."

"Of course it does."

"James. Whatever's in there, I don't want it. Honestly."

Duncan paused to take in his reaction. James' did not look too surprised.

"Give it to Nat or something," Duncan added.

James' hand gripped the envelope in a way that crinkled the paper a bit, and then he let his hand fall gently to his side. Without a word, he stood up, his back toward Duncan, still for a moment. Then, he briskly placed the envelope on Duncan's bedside table and left without another glance.

After a good minute had passed, when he knew no one was by the door, Duncan reached over and grabbed it. Printed in James' unsteady handwriting was written: *for Duncan*.

1974

DAD'S RIGHT HAND REACHED toward the treetops, his left lay softly on his son's head. It was sultry that day, yet the cold water bit at both of their legs as it rushed by, tempting Duncan to forgo his smile.

"Do you believe you're trapped in your sins and need deliverance?" Dad said, resounding enough so the congregation that was standing on and around the makeshift bridge could listen in.

Duncan nodded.

"Do you," he continued, "have a repentant heart? A heart ready to submit to Jesus, the only

Son of God—who is God? Do you believe He became a man in order to restore you back to the Father? That He came to rescue you from the consequence of your sins by living the perfect life, making up for all your lack? And also by bearing the wrath of God in your place so that you may live in loving obedience to Him forever?"

Again, he nodded.

"Do you believe that the Father rose Jesus up on the third day so that He could also give His chosen ones new life? And that He sent His Holy Spirit to live inside you and seal you for the day of salvation?"

Yes, Duncan was sure of it.

After these questions, his dad lowered his hand and bent down to meet his son's eyes. Dad's boomy voice suddenly subsided, this time speaking just so Duncan could hear.

"But do you *want* Him?"

Their eyes lingered on one another. "Yes," Duncan whispered back with confidence.

Dad grinned, taking one last glimpse of him before rising to his feet again and lifting his hand in the air a second time.

"Well, then. Because you have professed a repentant heart full of faith in God and His Son, in the name of the Father, the Son, and the Holy Spirit, I welcome you into the Kingdom. As you go under, this shows that you have died with Christ. As you come up, this signifies you are raised a new man. A new man with a new life— Christ's life. And because His life is rich and never ends, so will yours be. No one will be able to take this truth away from you. Your salvation is secure."

The two of them went on their knees. Dad moved the placement of his hands to sturdy Duncan as he guided him into the stinging waters and pulled him back out again. In the next moment, they were squeezing one another. Whether it was out of joy or to find some sudden warmth, Duncan was not sure.

NAT SAT ON HIS MOM'S LAP, avidly playing with her hair to the point that the congregants were beginning to look her way, and she had to constantly redirect his arms elsewhere.

"Sorry," she finally apologized to the other

men and women who were sitting closely in lawn chairs on the grass of their backyard, "he's fascinated with my hair, now that it's coming back in."

"As I was saying," Dad interjected, who was standing up from his chair as he told his story, "its eyes are as dark and glassy as black coals. Its coat as wild and grisly as the beast itself! And it roams among these very trees...So it has been told."

"Honey," Mom said, "You're going to scare the kids. We were just in the woods for Duncan's baptism."

"It's true!"

She noticed his hand holding an almost depleted beer bottle, as well as the two others that lay empty on the grass beside his feet, making a note to herself.

"So you've seen it?" She said, smirking confidently as if she had found the loose thread of his claim.

Dad immediately pointed to a congregant from within the gathering. "Tell them," he said, urging the man.

"That's why I keep my rifle close," joked a

low-toned, somewhat sandy voice.

Mom looked off to the side to see who spoke. "James, you're not serious?"

"But it's been a few years. Only saw it once from a distance. Could have been my imagination, if anything."

"Must have been," she asserted, crossing her arms. "We don't have bears in this region."

"There are exceptions to every rule," Dad inserted.

"Well, anyway," Mom said, "Duncan. Take your brother to get a drink. And then go play."

She frowned at Dad slightly while scooting Nat off her and handing him to Duncan.

The boys ambled to the beverage table, one of Duncan's ears still intent on hearing the rest of Dad's bear story. However, it was momentarily halted by Zack's sudden appearance.

"So…That was cool, I guess," said Zack. "Like, swimming, huh?"

"Not really," Duncan said, reaching for two plastic cups. "So, when are *you* getting baptized?"

"Your dad said my profession isn't credible or something. Said we'd talk about it again later in the year maybe. He wants to counsel me, he said."

Nat held his cup as Duncan began pouring the punch into it.

"What does that mean, 'not credible'?" he asked Zack, glancing over.

Zack shrugged unconcernedly.

"*Heeeyyy!* You're making me *stickyyy!*" Nat squealed.

Apparently, Duncan hadn't been paying close enough attention to what he was doing. Nat's punch had flowed over the brim of the cup, onto his hands, and down both his forearms. Oops.

Duncan's hands reached for some napkins, but none were on the table.

"Hey," Duncan said, turning to Zack, "can you go in the house real quick and get some paper towels?"

Immediately, Zack hasted toward the kitchen, opened the back door, and scanned the countertops cluttered with crockpots and an assortment of foiled dishes. In the corner by the coffeemaker, Zack spotted a thinning roll of paper towels and grabbed it. On his way back, however, his eyes followed the corridor that led to the bathroom. Through the considerable gap in the door, the vanity reflected two people kissing insatiably. Zack's eyes grew so broad that it seemed as if they could roll out of his sockets. The man was his father, the woman certainly not his mother.

Between the rough and disheveled kissing, the woman opened her eyes and at once found Zack gaping at them down the hallway.

"Bill," she said in soft horror. "Who's that?"

Zack and his father met eyes with dark and stinging tension.

Back at the beverage table, Duncan was waiting for Zack to pop around the corner of the house to try and scare him. Though, he noticed he and Nat had stood there for a considerably long time.

"Looks like you got yourself a situation here," said a man behind them.

Duncan turned around to see that it was James.

"Yeah," he answered.

James rubbed Duncan's hair affectionately. He smiled back at him.

"You need help with that?" James asked, looking at the sugary mess.

"No, Zack's coming back with some towels."

"Ah. Well, if you excuse me, then. Just going to go around you. Get myself a cup."

He did just that. James poured himself a cup and smiled at Nat and Duncan before trodding back toward the clutter of lawn chairs.

Moments later, Zack stumbled toward the two.

"Where are the paper towels?" Duncan said.

Just as he had said those words, Duncan noticed Zack's dad open the kitchen door suspiciously and gaze in their direction. There was a ruffling of the bathroom curtain, and a figure cloaked translucently behind it.

A moment later, Duncan stopped hearing the sound of his dad's voice. He looked over to see Dad turn toward the house with a surmising expression. Zack's father glanced around at the scene he was causing and hid himself inside again. Soon after, Dad put down his beer and, trying not to seem noticeably distressed, strode determinedly toward the back kitchen door.

1980

THE TWO WERE FIXED on the brick building as James' pickup pulled into the parking spot.

"Is this it?" Duncan said.

"This is it."

They spent the next twenty minutes systematizing how to move everything from the bed to the dorm room, then began placing the boxes on the sidewalk next to the black pickup. There was one box in particular that was difficult to get down.

A girl—a girl with noticeably dark brown curls that spiraled down to her shoulders and eyes resembling emeralds—was walking up the sidewalk just a short distance from them.

Her eyes flicked up Duncan's way, causing his own to dart elsewhere.

"Do you and your dad want a hand?" she asked.

"Oh," Duncan answered quickly, "he's not my dad."

An unusual hiccup happened as her eyes motioned from Duncan to James and then back again.

"Don't you need to unpack, too?" James said to her.

"I came in yesterday."

Duncan's eyes rested back on her.

"Are you sure you two don't need help?" she said.

"No, I think we're okay, thanks," James said with a smile. "Aren't we, Duncan? Are we all right?"

Duncan turned toward James, who had been watching him become fixated on her.

"Yeah," Duncan said. "We're fine."

A few guys opened the door for him and

James as they finished lugging the boxes to Duncan's room. James didn't stay too long after that, though. He sat on Duncan's mattress for a minute or two to catch his breath, then stood up again.

"I want to show you something before I go," he said to Duncan.

Both of them walked down the antiquated hallway and into a common area that cried out for a remodel. A few other college guys were in there talking amongst themselves at what seemed to be a precarious-looking wooden table. Though, James didn't go up to them. Instead, he led Duncan to a long wall painted matte black, resembling a large chalkboard. On it were written many names.

"Well, can you find him?" James said.

Duncan scanned the tapestry of signatures—there were far too many to give great attention to—but his eyes didn't miss it. The signature was bold and distinct: *Pat McLaughlin '59*.

He fell completely silent, forgetting how to make out words as he gazed admiringly at the calligraphy. Slowly, Duncan approached the signature and stroked his fingers over the painted surface. Moments elapsed before he turned back to James.

"He was here," Duncan said in disbelief.

"I said he went here," James replied, his arms folded, making out a grin.

Duncan's eyes lowered to the floor, his stunned appearance now turned solemn. "Why did Mom keep that a secret?"

"…I don't know."

"I never knew he went to this college. Not until *you* mentioned it to me."

"Listen," James said. "I'm sure she didn't keep it a secret. She probably just never had a reason to bring it up in conversation."

"After I ask for information on him…I think that'd be a perfect time."

The breeze from the open window died down to stagnancy as they stood there in silence. After giving one last cursory glance at the wall, Duncan placed his hand in his pocket and took out the envelope James had given him just the day before. He slipped it back into James' hand as he walked by him without a word.

For a moment, James remained statue-like.

Then, slowly turning over the envelope, he noticed the seal was not broken.

DUNCAN'S HAND GENTLY STROKED the spines of the old yearbooks gathered on one shelf near the far corner of the library. Once his finger lay softly over the year *1959*, he quickly slid it out from its resting place and brought it over to one of the study tables. His hands swiftly turned the pages until he saw him. There he was, his father, pictured above his name. His dad's eyes were squinted slightly, his lips wide, his teeth poking out a bit.

Duncan was there for a while, taking in the photograph, until he noticed in the corner of his eye the girl whom he had been momentarily captivated with a few weeks back. She was sitting at another study table near the other side of the library. Her eyes and hand were narrowed in on the black journal she had in front of her. He paused, taking her in like a photograph, before continuing to file through the yearbook.

When his gaze had floated upwards again a

few minutes later, she was gone, except that her journal lay closed on the desk by itself.

Duncan panned the library to see if she was around, but he heard no rustle nor saw movement through the gaps in the shelves of books.

Once again, he looked over at the unattended desk with the lonely journal on top. With slight hesitation, he closed his book, placed it back on the shelf with the other yearbooks, and went over to the journal to pick it up.

It was in his hand while Duncan walked around the library, but she wasn't in the back. As he was about to walk out of the building, he found her talking with the librarian at the front desk.

"Hey," Duncan said as he went up to her.

She turned around. "Hey."

Noticing he held her black journal, she instinctively reached for it.

"You left this," He said, giving it to her.

"Thank you…"

"Duncan."

"Rachel," she said. Though her mouth didn't widen, it seemed as if she were smiling. "Hey, you're the one I saw on the first day. Did you and your dad get all unpacked okay—? I mean, I'm sorry. You said he's not your dad?"

"Stepfather."

"Ah…Well, thank you, Duncan," she held the journal up briefly, "for this."

"You bet."

Duncan's feet began to move, but her words stopped him. "You know," she continued, "I've noticed you spending some time in the library looking at old yearbooks. I have a friend on the yearbook team if you want to meet her."

"Oh. No, I'm not looking to be on the team."

"You seem pretty enthralled by them."

"Just…my dad's in them. My real dad. Learning more about him, that's all."

"That's interesting. I thought you were looking at pictures of your stepdad."

"What do you mean?"

"I thought he looked familiar. Just the other day, when I was helping my friend look through some old yearbooks to get a feel for what direction she wants to go this year, I saw some photos of him."

"In the yearbook?"

"You didn't know that?" she said.

"I didn't see anything."

"Maybe it was just someone who looked like him."

"Well, he never said a word to me about it."

"And you said you're learning about your dad, too? You don't know much about him?"

While he believed silence could have provided a sufficient answer, Duncan decided to speak up. "He's not around long enough for me to ask him."

"Couldn't you call him up?"

He did let the silence answer this time.

"Well," she said. "There aren't any yearbooks at home?"

"No. We got rid of a lot of stuff over the years. I guess that was my mom's way of starting over."

"She should have some information, at least, no?"

"She doesn't like to talk about him anymore... Well, she used to. Just—not since James."

"Your stepfather," she inserted as if it were a question.

Duncan nodded.

"I don't know," she said, "I would still ask. I

mean, she's your mom, right? And your dad. Well, he's your father."

"Yeah."

"Well, you let me know how it goes, okay, Duncan?"

With that, Duncan knew the conversation was over and that it was time for him to finally move his feet. So he did. Though, a part of him wanted to stay.

1974

THE NIGHT WORE ON, and the neighborhood seemed to finally settle. That was, except for the two boys. Zack sat with a glassy expression, sitting on the front porch step for a good long while. Eventually, Duncan joined him, placing his hand over his shoulder. They sat like that for a time, letting the nocturnal sounds become the conversation before the front door was opened.

"Zack," Mom said softly, "Your mother called. She wants you home, okay?"

"How about Dad?" he said.

Mom hesitated. "Let me take you home.

Going through those woods at night just scares me."

"I'll just take the streets," Zack said.

"Really, I can take you home."

"I'm okay, Mrs. McLaughlin. It's just a few blocks away."

"Well, okay. I'll call her and let her know you're heading there now. You have a good night, Zack. Come back tomorrow if you want."

Zack nodded, then stood up. Something seemed odd about him, though. His usually confident posture had slouched into something unnatural.

Duncan stood up also. "I'll go with him," he told Mom resolutely.

"Just to the tracks," she said.

Once she had resigned herself to the kitchen, they began walking down the light-spotted street.

"Wanna race?" Duncan said, speaking up.

"Not really," Zack said.

"Come on. To the tracks. Just two streets away."

Zack shivered as if his words had a wintry sting to them.

"You're the one who wanted to walk home," Duncan continued. "It'll help you get over your fear of train tracks, anyway."

"I'm not scared."

"No train is going to hit you just because you step on it. My dad says believing stuff like that's just silly superstition."

"I said I'm not scared!"

"Well, good. Prove it."

And so it was that Duncan and Zack stood in the middle of the road under one of the light posts. Their hands met the warm, worn blacktop, their feet poised for a competition. They counted down together, and as if a gun had gone off in the middle of their sleepy town, they were off.

Darting from light post to light post, they stayed neck-and-neck. Past the first stop sign and down the bend, the two couldn't necessarily see their own feet. The darkness constantly hindered their vision. Though, they could see it in the distance—the tracks. As it grew larger in view, Zack slipped behind.

Meanwhile, two beams of light appeared on the other side approaching much quicker than the tracks themselves. A black pickup was headed in their direction. It thumped over the tracks and passed them, slowing down as it went around the bend.

"There!" Duncan said confidently. "We made it!"

Zack came to a crawl as he met the steel rails, stopping just before it. Duncan was waiting on the other side.

"Come on," Duncan called out as if they were a hundred yards apart.

He stood frozen, looking down at it. When Duncan noticed Zack was hypnotized, he walked over the rails and took out his hand.

"Grab it," he said to him. And Zack did. "Don't let go."

Duncan guided him slowly over the first steel rail, along the pavement, and passed the second. He kept gripping his hand, even though he was safely on the other side.

"Hey, I gotta go," Duncan said. "See you tomorrow?"

He nodded despondently. They hugged and went their separate ways that evening—Zack to his house and Duncan to his own. It took a little while longer to get home than to the tracks, since Duncan strolled rather than sprinted. But as he rounded the bend and came to the crest of the hill to see that black pickup sitting in his driveway, he immediately picked up the pace.

As he cornered the driveway and made his way toward the house door, Duncan glanced over to see the pickup empty, except for a hunting rifle hidden in the dark on the passenger side. Before he could wonder whose it was, a man exited on the front porch—it was James. The two met eyes, James' head turning around to keep eye contact for a moment more as they passed each other. James didn't smile.

Inside, Duncan's gaze suddenly shifted onto the sight of another man lying front down on the couch. This man's hair looked damp and frazzled, his face hidden.

"He's okay, Honey," a voice spoke with hesitancy.

Mom appeared from the kitchen with a moist washcloth in her hand.

"...What happened?" Duncan asked,

frightened.

"Your father's passed out. Just go upstairs and get ready for bed."

"I can help."

"It's all right. Thanks, Sweetie. He'll wake up in a little bit. Don't you worry, Hon."

Not another word was spoken that night. Duncan's heart shook quietly, his eyes unable to pull themselves from that scene as he ambled up the steps.

1980

NAT STARED AT THE THANKSGIVING DAY parade silently playing on the television in the other room.

"Pass me the mashed potatoes, Hon," Mom said to Nat.

He stole one last glance at the TV set before shifting his attention at last to the food before him. He lifted the bowl and leaned over that extra, empty plate so Mom could reach it.

"Not hungry?" she said, now directing her comment to Duncan.

He didn't shrug or move his head. Instead,

Duncan's eyes drifted off her toward the ceiling, as if he was considering what she said.

"He's thinking about that girl," James said, grinning.

"I didn't know there's a girl," Mom said, her voice immediately an octave higher.

"There's not," Duncan said, his ears reddening.

"Why didn't you let me know?"

"There's no girl."

"Why didn't you ask her out?" James pressed. "Just asking. That's all."

"I told you, we're not even friends, really."

"It's okay to like her," Mom added, her eyes laser-focused on her son.

"Mom, please…"

"Okay. My mouth is shut."

"It's not that big of a deal," Duncan told them, hoping this particular conversation would move in a different direction.

"You didn't even tell us her name," Nat added.

"Nat. Drop it, all right, Sweetie?"

"Forgive me," said James. "I was just curious if you saw her since." He took a bite of what was on his plate and looked at Mom. "She came up to us and asked if she could help on move-in day."

"I see," she said. "You think you'll have another class with her?"

"It might be likely," Duncan said, though clearly uncomfortable at this point.

"How so?" Mom went on.

"I'm just not hungry. Is it all right that I be done?"

Mom's eyes peered concernedly down the table at Duncan. "…Sure."

With that, he stood up and went upstairs to his room, now making two empty place settings.

THREE BOXES WERE STACKED LIKE A PYRAMID, carried by Mom as she walked up from the basement and set them down with a sigh. After taking a moment to catch her breath, she scooted them across the downstairs floor and into the living room where some others were already opened.

"Mom?" Duncan said cautiously as he approached her from behind.

She peered around—surprised, it seemed.

"Oh. Honey. Why didn't you help? Can't you see they're a little heavy for me?"

"I just came downstairs," I told her. "What are you doing with all these Christmas boxes already?"

"Rummaging through some of them. I think it's time we take a lighter approach on the decorations this year. Simple. I like simple."

"Mom?"

"Yes, Sweetie."

"Mom," he repeated like a scratched record, his hands beginning to clam up a bit. "I want to know more about Dad."

"Oh, Honey. Oh. I...I'm sorry—

"It's been six years," he said. "Six years without him has been hard enough. But what about his stuff? What about the pictures? Records of him?"

"Duncan, you seem very possessed by this desire to know."

"He's my dad. Of course I am."

"I know, Sweetheart. I know. But after six years of him being gone? You just decided to start searching?"

There was a snap to her words.

"He came to see me," Duncan told her flatly.

Mom changed her stance, her eyes widening like a parallax effect.

"When?"

"At the wedding," he told her. "He didn't stay long."

"You saw him again?"

"Not since then," Duncan folded his arms. "I'd ask him these questions if I could."

"Why didn't you tell me he came back?"

"It doesn't matter."

"Honey. Look, it's been hard for all of us. I need you to know that. I just don't—I don't know if I can help you."

"Why? Because six years is too soon?"

"Ducan."

"Will twenty even be enough?"

Her eyes glinted, though Duncan was unsure of the exact reason why, yet he surmised by the way her tried smile vanished that she was remembering.

"…Maybe not," she said, almost in a whisper.

1974

His hands slowly pushed on his bedroom door so the sound wouldn't alarm his parents that he was awake. Duncan created a sliver in the doorway, allowing the conversation that was rising like hot air from the downstairs below to waft into the room.

"I don't understand," he could hear Mom say with a pained sigh. "You're supposed to be helping him."

"I *am* helping him," said another voice, though raspier and slurred.

"Looks like you're trying to help yourself. And

you're not doing a very good job at it, mind you."

"Don't give me that."

"What?"

"I know what I am."

"What are you then? Tell me. Are you not my husband? Are not the boys your children? For heaven's sake, you're supposed to be counseling Bill. How can you do that when *you* need it?"

"He's the one who wants to meet. He's got issues, Sarah. It's affecting his marriage. And Zack knows now."

"It's affecting more than *his* family."

"I'm fine."

A long stretch of silence almost made Duncan believe the conversation was over. But then Mom responded, her voice sounding tired now.

"No, you're not fine. That's why you get this way. That's why you won't stop."

"I can stop…What?"

"How can you stand here and continue to tell me that you're fine? It's past midnight and you, the pastor, must be driven home by one of your own congregants. Again."

"Don't use that."

"I shouldn't remind you that you're a pastor? It's true."

"I'm fine," he was determined to repeat, though it seemed that was all he could think of saying.

"You lie. Yet you believe it. How can you be so convinced like your father—

"I'm not like my father!" his voice escalated.

Duncan noticed the conversation went silent for yet another moment.

"Well, you better get to bed," Mom told him with finality; her voice now died down to almost a whisper, forcing Duncan to lean his head out the door to catch what she was saying. "It's now the Lord's Day, and you have a sermon to preach in a few hours."

"You want me to leave, don't you?" the raspy, slurred voice said, a sharpness to it. "Sarah, come back."

"Talk to me when you're sober. Then maybe we can have a real, sensible conversation."

Duncan could hear her footsteps hasting toward the stairs, yet as quickly as he closed the door and put his head on his pillow again, the door swung back open with insistence.

"Nat!" Duncan exclaimed quietly, trying not to appear surprised. "Knock first."

Without any thought, Nat went and sat on his bed so determinedly that Duncan believed nothing would make him stand up.

"They're being loud again," Nat said.

Noticing his eyes widening and face trembling, Duncan's rigid disposition softened quite instantly. He placed his hand gently on Nat's shoulder and lightened his voice.

"Here," Duncan said. "Let's pray."

He placed his hands together in the center of his lap, bowed his head, and saw in the corner of his eye that Nat was mirroring everything he was doing.

"Heavenly Father—

"Heavenly Father," Nat repeated.

Duncan paused, then said, "No, I'll just—

"No, I'll just," Nat mimicked again.

Duncan paused for a second time, though longer than before.

"Let me pray, Nat, okay?"

He nodded his head and closed his eyes,

waiting very still.

"Heavenly Father," Duncan began. "Thank you for Mom and Dad. We know you love them. Stop their fighting. Help them love each other again. And keep Nat and me from waking up in the middle of the night. In Jesus' name. Amen—

As Duncan was ending, Nat inserted with great speed, "AndIWannaBBGunForChristmas-Amen!"

"Hey! Jesus isn't Santa Claus…Come on. Back to bed."

But Nat wasn't moving. His eyes seemed to grow wider, his posture more somber. Though, it might have just been Duncan imagining it.

Regardless, he knew what this meant.

"Just tonight," Duncan said with soft firmness. "And stay on your side. I literally fell out of bed the last time."

Nat quickly went under Duncan's covers and said nothing. Only when Duncan joined him, his hand mildly wrapping around his little brother and his body drawing close to his, did Nat finally shut his eyes.

1981

DUNCAN SAT ON HIS DORM ROOM BED, his eyes roaming the open Bible on his lap, periodically closing them to meditate on what he had just read. As time went along, though, he found it more difficult to concentrate. Eventually, the noise that seemed to find its way through his window reached his ears so persistently that he was forced to turn toward it. At first, all he noticed were the clumps of snow heaping their way down toward the scene below. But as he approached the window, Duncan noticed folks on the white-covered lawn, making a lively afternoon in the cold. He couldn't help but smile.

He gazed at the living picture for quite some time, and just as he was about to pull away, Duncan caught a glimpse of a girl alone on a bench just outside his window. She was writing in a black-covered book with her mittens on.

Rachel.

He did not spare another minute before lacing up his boots and putting on his overcoat. She was still writing by the time he had made it out of the dormitory entrance.

She looked up to see who was coming her way.

"Duncan?" Rachel said hesitantly.

"Uh…Yeah," he said back, even more hesitantly. "Hey."

"Hey."

"Aren't you cold?"

"I was actually getting a little hot in my room," she said, smiling. "You know, there's no way to adjust the thermostat. They seem to always turn up the heat. I guess that's a good thing. Better than no heat. Besides, my roommate's making too much noise anyway, so…" she trailed off for a moment. "Did you want to sit?"

She made room before for Duncan could answer, so naturally he felt obliged to go over to her and sit down on the frozen bench.

"Do you write poems in here?" he asked, peering over her shoulder.

"You seem oddly curious," she said.

"Oh, I'm sorry. I didn't mean—

"It's all right. It's not a secret—Really. I usually do write poems, yes. I know, right? So cliché. The president of the Poet Society just so happens to write poetry. But I also write psalms. And prayers."

"You write prayers?"

"That's what I'm writing right now."

"I never heard of anyone writing down their prayers before," I said.

"Really? You've never heard of *The Valley of Vision*? Or *The Book of Common Prayer*? Or of any liturgy? Do you know what a liturgy is?"

"Well, I guess so."

"You should try it. Some of the most powerful prayers are those written down. I believe so, anyway."

As Rachel spoke, Duncan's vision slowly

shifted from her and onto an array of unclear thoughts. A distant, childish scream crept in and faded just as quickly.

"Are you all right?" Rachel said with mild concern.

"…Yeah."

"Is it a migraine?"

"Something like that," Duncan fibbed. "I've had it for a while now. Six years, at least."

"You want something for it? I've got something in my purse that might help with that."

"No, that's all right."

"Are you sure?"

Her bright green eyes were unflinching.

Duncan placed his hand on his forehead, rubbing it gently, discerning if his head really was hurting. Then suddenly, his hand was seized by hers. She looked it over on her lap. A scar was stitched visibly along the palm of his hand.

"Duncan," Rachel said, now visibly distraught.

"It's not what you think."

"…Duncan."

"I promise," he said, trying to reassure her.

"Really. It's okay. I'm okay."

Rachel gave him an unsure look and rubbed his scar ever so gently with her delicate fingers. Then, she rolled up one of her sleeves, turned over her forearm, and placed her wrist next to his hand. She, too, had a scar stitched a long way.

"I know what that means, Duncan," Rachel said.

"Rachel?!" he exclaimed. "Are you all right?"

"Yeah," she said, putting her sleeve down again, her cheeks flushed, and not from the cold. "That was years ago. When I was lost."

Duncan made sure that her eyes were fully fixed on his before he spoke.

"These aren't the same type of scars," he said. "Yours and mine."

"…Okay, then."

With that, they sat in silence, letting the laughter of those around them fill the conversation, unsure of one another. But Duncan could sense they both were glad to be in each other's company.

1974

ZACK AND DUNCAN SAT TOGETHER on that particular Sunday. They did not usually have the opportunity. Over time, it was made apparent to both of them that their mothers didn't want them close enough to cause distractions. Though, that day was different. They even let the two boys sit one pew in front of them, all by themselves.

Zack's father was not there like he often was. In fact, his brazen absence seemed like the clear reason why Zack and his mom didn't want to sit alone.

Dad, of course, did not sit down. He was

preaching, as always. And he was finishing up, Duncan could tell.

"We constantly look up toward the everlasting goal," he said in conclusion to his hour-long sermon, "where the prize dwells in the land of the living. Where the Son has the saints rule with Him as they were meant to from the beginning, and where sin and death have no power over the one who trusts in the Lord—in Yahweh. Therefore, their sufferings are inconsequential to the joy of their salvation and sure hope that one day their faith will become sight…With all this to consider, let's pray."

And so they did.

SOON AFTERWARD, ONCE THOSE in the pews had all strolled slowly out of the building, Zack and Duncan quickly found themselves in the woods, skipping rocks on the water's edge. They didn't even bother to change their Sunday clothes.

"Noticed your dad wasn't at service today," Duncan said awkwardly.

"Is that really news?" Zack said flatly.

"What'd you do? Trip or something?"

"What?"

Duncan pointed to his own face, indicating that there was something on Zack's. And there *was* —a mighty dark bruise grazed his cheekbone.

"Oh," Zack said embarrassingly. "Yeah."

"How'd you do that?"

"These dumb rocks. I hate this place."

"Should we stop throwing them, then?" Duncan said.

"No. They deserve to be beaten to the ground."

Duncan's eyes narrowed in on him, trying to figure out what he meant by those words.

"You all right?" Duncan asked, his voice mixed with concern and confusion.

"Yeah, I'm fine," Zack said, trying to sound as if he really was but failing quite obviously.

Zack threw another rock—hastily this time— forcing it to plop heavily into the crick. At first, Duncan wasn't sure what that meant, but he continued to skip them. Zack slowly made an effort to do the same, but it appeared as if his pensive disposition got the better of him. And he soon stopped altogether.

In the end, Duncan stopped, too. Cautiously, his feet made their way over to Zack's. He gently placed his hand on Zack's shoulder and guided him to a sitting position. They sat beside each other near the water, shoulder-to-shoulder, as Zack's eyes grew red and his nose became thin and runny. Duncan could feel his friend's body rising and falling as if crying silently to himself. But Zack spoke quite resolutely.

"Why do you care so much?" he said.

Duncan didn't know if that was a compliment or an accusation.

"Because you're my brother," Duncan told him plainly.

"No, I'm not."

"Of course you are."

"I'm not even blood," Zack said.

"Blood isn't everything."

"But it's enough. That's all you have to be is blood."

"Blood doesn't make a brother, you know."

"Then what does?"

Duncan listened to the stream as he gave the

question some thought.

"I don't know," he said eventually. "Seeing each other every day. Going to school. Sitting with each other at lunch. Playing around in the woods."

"Is that all?" Zack said, unconvinced.

"Sharing secrets," Duncan continued. "Things we wouldn't tell anyone else. Being there, even when it's hard. And showing the other one we care. That we love them."

Duncan began to notice that Zack's eyes were floating in every direction, which never managed to land on him. Zack's body fidgeted here and there, making Duncan suspect something else on his mind. So Duncan resigned himself to remain still, his eyes locked on his friend, waiting patiently.

"*What?*" Zack said defensively, yet trying to hide it with a smile.

Duncan blinked at him.

Zack, his face now a bit flushed, stood up. Duncan watched him amble around him with his hands in his pockets, his feet kicking up dried leaves and some earth.

Duncan resolved to stand up as well, though

decidedly did not amble. Instead, he planted his feet firmly on the ground and put his hands down to his sides like a soldier or a statue. Zack's eyes came to rest on him again, but Duncan was not smiling. He looked rather serious, which irked Zack.

"Stop," Zack said, mirroring Duncan's solemn expression.

"*You* stop."

"No. *You* stop!"

Duncan's eyes kept watch on Zack, who now faced him, his body still.

"You gonna tell me?" Duncan offered.

"Tell you what?"

Duncan sighed. "Whatever."

He turned his back on his friend and began walking toward the bridge. Zack's hardened demeanor suddenly melted to worry and sadness, and just as he was about to speak up, Duncan turned around and said, "That bruise…didn't come from the rocks, did it?"

Zack stood there as if he had been caught, his bulging eyes reflecting the fear within him.

1981

"YOUR FATHER'S A PASTOR?" Rachel asked, her voice showing interest.

They were looking out onto a glassy lake just beyond the campus, the morning sky reflecting on the water. She sat close to Duncan on the dock as their toes dipped lazily in the water. Though they were fishing, they hadn't caught anything. Their attention was given to conversation.

"Not anymore," Duncan told her. "Sorry, maybe I shouldn't have talked about him."

"No, *I'm* sorry," she said. "I didn't mean to press."

When Rachel saw he had nothing to add, she shifted the discussion. "So you fish back home? Since you said you had a crick in your backyard?"

"This is my roommate's," Duncan said, referring to the fishing pole he held awkwardly in his hands.

Immediately, she grinned. "That's not what you're supposed to say," she said.

"What?"

"You're trying to impress me, right?"

No words came out of Duncan's mouth.

"You invite a girl to go fishing with you. You don't just say you've never fished before."

"I never said I don't fish."

"So you fish?" she asked rhetorically.

Duncan's eyes fell from looking at her.

"Don't worry," Rachel went on. "I didn't come for the fish."

He looked back up to find her staring at him. He stared back. They stayed that way for a while, but eventually, Duncan felt a pull, an invisible tug. And he leaned in for it—a kiss.

Rachel backed away, but he zeroed in so intently that he caught her lips like a fish on a hook. After the briefest of moments, she broke free. Although, she was unaware that her black journal was right next to her—and it ended up flopping into the water.

"Duncan…" she groaned.

After an embarrassing glance, Rachel tried extending her arm toward the lake.

"I'm sorry," Duncan apologized, his ears suddenly red hot.

He noticed her becoming unsteady as she reached farther out her hand, grabbing the wooden dock post to keep her balance.

"Here," Duncan said. "I'll get it."

He took out his fishing pole from the water in haste, but instead of landing back on the dock, the line found itself in Rachel's hair.

"Duncan!" she gasped.

He tried to safely tug the pole out of the nest of hair, but as he was doing so, Rachel lost her balance entirely and splashed into the lake. Resigned to the providence given to her, she retrieved the book and placed it back on the dock defeatedly. Duncan reached out his hand toward, who was still treading in the water, but she ignored it and simply used her own strength to get back onto the wooden surface.

The expression on her face gave away her miserable state as she flipped through the soaked pages of her journal.

Without another word, Duncan slowly stood up with cheeks too red to show and walked off with the two fishing poles. Rachel watched Duncan exit before continuing to mourn over the book she had lost to the lake.

THE DAYS GREW WARMER and the trees thicker, though Duncan's embarrassment didn't go away. He'd find Rachel here and there on the small campus. Sometimes, it appeared as if she wanted to talk. Though, Duncan couldn't bear to look at her. Every time, he went right past, but she caught him one time as he was hurrying toward the dormitory.

She was sitting on that same bench they shared just a few months before. Duncan looked the other way as he walked on by.

"Duncan," she said loud enough to be certain

he heard her.

So he turned around—there was no other choice, it appeared.

"Hey," said Duncan sheepishly.

The two looked at each other awkwardly, but Duncan eventually interpreted Rachel's stare to mean *come here*. So he did.

She made room for him, and he sat down next to her. His eyes hung low, waiting, yet unsure what she would say. As he may have suspected, she opened up her journal that she seemed to always have with her.

"May I?" she said.

When Duncan gave a short nod, his eyes still refusing to meet hers, she looked down at the words on the page and read them aloud:

> *There she lay atop the muck*
> *Of all her shame that made her stuck*
> *She cursed herself forevermore*
> *Far underneath the darkest shore*
>
> *The cold steel walls were tall and grim*
> *Those rusted bars and chains of sin*

They kept her there 'til her last breath
Which never ceased nor gave her rest

The Father's grace she could not plea
To cure her wounds and set her free
Instead she wallowed in her tears
Which filled her lungs from all those years

But mighty is our God to save
That poor lone girl who dug her grave
He reached His hand far down below
To raise her up and have her know

His love goes deeper than the sea
His hand of grace will always be
On her so she won't be alone
The Father's love will bring her home

Rachel closed her journal softly and placed it safely between her lap and her hands.

"That's beautiful," said Duncan shyly.

"I wrote that a long while back—sometime after I made those scars."

She turned to face him, her eyes unflinching.

"I wasn't upset. Surprised, that's all."

"Which part?" Duncan asked.

"Both, I guess."

"I shouldn't have done that."

"But you don't need to avoid me, either, if that's what you've been trying to do." She looked out on the lawn and continued. "Why are you so hard on yourself? You know, you don't need to keep to yourself all the time, as if that will make up for what happened."

"I don't get it," said Duncan. "I ruined your journal. Whichever one that was. Is this it?"

"No…"

"I shouldn't have kissed you."

"It's okay, Duncan. You don't need to apologize."

Even though her words soothed him in some small way, Rachel could clearly see he was not all settled.

"What's the matter?" she said. "Seriously."

Duncan's eyes floated away from her. She noticed this and, after a while of quiet inspection, carefully took his scarred hand, interlacing her fingers with mine. Rachel put her other hand around his arm and gently laid her head on his shoulder. And in that moment, his heart felt somehow lighter.

1974

DUNCAN TRIED TO KEEP the wind from turning the pages of his Bible, but it didn't seem to do any good. The water was also a bit upset as it winded along the whistling forest. He was alone, but not for long. The sound of footsteps approaching was heard on the other side of the crick from the direction of the church building.

Looking intently at the brush in front of him, Duncan found Zack emerge along the path. It only took a moment to find a few new bruises grazing his body.

Duncan closed his Bible and rose to his feet.

The two boys stood on either end of the crick, Zack looking melancholy while Duncan was noticeably distressed.

"I'm telling you, Zack, you need to tell your mom what he's doing!" said Duncan firmly. "It's only been a week, and I can see those bruises from over here."

"Yeah, you can't really hide these, can you?" Zack said, trying to sound lighthearted but failing at it.

Two more had appeared on his face and one near his elbow since the last time the boys saw each other.

"I'm serious!" Duncan exclaimed.

"Dude, I told you. She knows. I'm the one trying to keep him away from *her*."

"Well, you need to tell someone who'll do something about it."

There were bags under Zack's eyes, and a wave of humiliation and fear that radiated from him swept over Duncan. It was hard for him to witness, to simply stand and watch his friend break down.

At first, Duncan stood there like an onlooker.

But eventually, he crossed into the water, approaching Zack slowly. The two were now only an arm's length from each other.

"Please let me tell my dad," Duncan said softly. "I promise you, your dad won't find out and try to hurt you—

"He's sending us away."

"Huh?"

"To Iowa," Zack said miserably.

"Iowa?" Duncan repeated in disbelief. "What's in Iowa?"

"Exactly."

"Are you saying you're all leaving together?"

"Now. That's why I came. I guess he's afraid people like your dad will start to notice all my bruises. And Mom's. He tried to keep me at home, that's why I haven't seen you for a while. He doesn't know I'm here. He said I couldn't tell anybody."

"You're leaving now?"

"He's probably trying to find me. I can't stay long. If he finds me out of the house…"

"Wait up," Duncan said as Zack began to back away.

He collected his thoughts as he waded back into the water, bending down and placing his hand along the riverbed. There, his fingers found a sharp, slated rock.

"What are you doing?!" Zack exclaimed as he saw blood coming from Duncan's palm as he sliced it.

"Brothers, right? Let's make it last."

Duncan handed him the rock. Zack looked it over suspiciously. As he noticed Duncan's palm becoming more red, though, he decided to take it and run it down his own.

Without any more delay, they clasped their wounded hands together, refusing to let go.

"Brothers," Zack said wearily.

"By blood," Duncan added.

A few drops landed on Duncan's Bible, which he had put on the ground when he approached him. Zack, observing this, grew somber again.

"Duncan?"

"Yeah."

"What does the Bible say about killing yourself?"

"What…?"

"I mean—would you still go to heaven?"

"Why are you asking that?" Duncan said with a trembling voice.

"ZACK!" yelled a distant, bitter voice.

Zack turned around in surprise. He heard the sound of angry footsteps bounding their direction.

"Is that your dad?" asked Duncan.

"*Ssshhh!!* Climb that tree. Don't make a sound."

"Zack!" cried the voice again, this time much closer. "Where are ya?!"

Immediately, Duncan ran off, motioned up the nearest tree, and hid himself as well as he could among the leaves. Just as he did so, a figure appeared.

"What are you doin' here?" Zack's dad said with a furrowed brow, looking down at his twelve-year-old son.

"Just standing here—

'Ya tryin' to go tell Duncan?"

"No."

"Ya tell Duncan what's been goin' on?"

"…No…"

A tense, hard slap streaked across Zack's face,

making tears fall from his eyes.

"Ya liar."

Zack shook his head, trembling with the kind of fear Duncan had never witnessed before.

"…This ain't yours."

Zack's dad pointed down at the Bible that lay a few feet away from them.

Zack didn't say anything. His concentration was on holding back more tears.

"Where is he?" His dad demanded.

"It was left here," Zack said, trying to sound convincing.

His dad's eyes narrowed in on him and eventually noticed his bloodied hand. He grasped his wrist tightly, causing Zack to wince.

"What'd ya do?"

"I had it in the water. Accidentally sliced it."

Zack's dad surveyed the woods as if paranoid. He never looked up.

He threw Zack's hand down and shoved his son toward the worn path. Both of them hastened toward the church building.

Duncan waited in the branches until he heard the pickup sputtering away. Then, he sprinted as fast as he could toward the church building.

Duncan's dad was at his desk, writing on a notepad, an open Bible at his side, when his son burst through the door.

"Duncan. Is everything okay?"

"Zack," he said with heavy breath.

"What about him?"

"He's gone."

"What do you mean, 'he's gone'?"

"His father sent them away."

Dad remained unconcerned. His eyes did not narrow in, his body remained relaxed.

"Did you hear me?" Duncan said to Dad, unsure if he had.

"I heard you, son."

"They're gone. He took them."

"Who took them?" Dad asked, still unmoved.

"Mr. Burns."

"That's his family. That's what families do. They leave together."

"But they don't wanna go."

"It doesn't have to be unanimously agreed upon."

"You're saying you knew they were leaving? To

Iowa!?"

"I have a friend up there. He's a pastor. I suggested to Bill that he—

"You told him to kidnap them?"

"Duncan. He's not kidnapping them."

"Zack said his dad doesn't want anyone to know."

"He's probably embarrassed," Dad said casually. "Look. You don't know the whole situation. But you can be assured that this is better for them. I've spoken many times with him. But I will admit that I didn't think he'd leave yet—"

"No, *you* don't know the whole situation!"

"And what's that?" said his dad with slight annoyance.

"Can't you tell he's been hurting them!"

"Hurting them?" He seemed surprised at this.

"I just saw it!" Duncan said as he began to cry. "There were bruises all over him. And now he's gone!"

Dad quickly went up to Duncan, knelt in front of him, and pressed his shoulders with his hands as his eyes appraised him. His son's body shook as the tears kept pouring down.

Dad, his eyes filled with determination, stood up and fetched the corded phone on his desk.

"What are you doing?" Duncan asked through his tears.

"Calling Pastor Dan. The one in Iowa."

"What is that going to do?"

"Duncan. Let me ring him."

Duncan fidgeted momentarily as he stood there, waiting for the phone to be answered. In a build-up of frustration, however, Duncan ran out of the office, down the sanctuary, through the entrance doors, and onto the lone street. There was nothing in sight—just a stretch of empty blacktop.

1981

JAMES STOOD ON THE WOODEN bridge alongside Nat. The two of them leaned over the rail, their fishing lines stretching all the way into the running stream. After a while, he placed his hand on Nat's shoulder, rubbing it affectionately.

"It's been a while," Nat said.

"You caught a decent one last time," James tried to reassure him.

"They're just not biting."

"You have to be patient, son. I know you're new at this, but if you have that, you'll be able to do much more than just fish."

"It's probably because the stream's low," said Duncan from afar.

James and Nat turned his way, unaware that he had partially hidden himself within the trees. Nat was the first to catch a glimpse of him, immediately throwing up a smile.

"Duncan!" he exclaimed, leaving his fishing pole to balance over the rail.

It took a moment more for James to find him, but once he saw the direction in which Nat was running, he, too, smiled wide.

"You're home a day early," James bellowed.

Duncan opened his arms to let Nat in, and they embraced for a good long while before meeting eyes.

"He missed you, can you tell?" James added.

James was now strolling toward Duncan with the two poles in his hand. Duncan could see James was beginning to open his arms for him, but he reached out his hand in time. James grabbed it hesitantly.

"Dad's been teaching me for a few weeks now," Nat said.

"Who?" Duncan said. "Wait, when did you

start calling him that?"

"I don't know. You haven't been home since Christmas. Sometime after then, I guess."

"Nat just started calling me 'Dad' one day," James explained. "Probably in March."

"I'm sure you calling him 'son' has something to do with it," Duncan told him flatly.

"I *am* his son," said Nat defensively. "Can't I call him 'Dad'?"

James and Duncan hooked stares, Duncan's narrowed and crossed.

"Mom wanted me to get you two for dinner. She said she was almost ready."

"Good," said Nat. "I haven't caught anything, and it's been an hour already."

Nat looked over to James to get his approval. When he nodded, Nat grabbed the two fishing poles from his hand and trodded off.

James opened his mouth to speak with Duncan, but Duncan had turned to follow Nat before a sound could come out.

*   *   *

NAT AND DUNCAN WALKED along the train tracks they used to do sometimes. Duncan rubbed his scarred hand, then put both of them in his pockets as he strode next to Nat on the wooden planks.

"Dad's been trying to teach me new things lately," Nat said as he attempted to balance on one of the rails. "He's started to play catch with me, and he says he's going to take me to a batting cage here soon."

"Why do you call him that?" Duncan said. "He's not your dad."

"But he is," Nat told him. "He legally adopted me. I've seen the papers."

"You think he's your dad just because of a piece of paper?"

"No. It just proves it."

"Just because he—

"Who else am I gonna call 'Dad'? Seriously. Do you want me to be fatherless? Is that what you want?"

"I'm just saying—you have a father."

"Yeah, well, not since I was seven. I'm fourteen now. I hardly remember anything about him."

"Hey, that's not true, is it? You have plenty of memories."

"Just because you're stuck in the past doesn't mean I have to be."

The wind picked up, causing the air to whistle as it rushed by their ears. "I know you're five years older than me, Duncan. And I know to you I'm still that seven-year-old, naive little kid who doesn't understand anything. But I do see things. I know you miss him. I know you have more memories with him than me. But I want a father just as much as you do."

Nat stopped, jumped off the rail, and began walking beside Duncan with his hands in his pockets, just like him. "I mean, I'm even old enough to have a girlfriend," Nat added.

"You have a girlfriend?" Duncan said, trying to smile even though all he had just said caused his stomach to tighten.

"No," he said shyly. "I just said I'm old enough."

"Well, I don't know if I agree."

"You don't have to. I just said I am."

"Well then," Duncan said, "there you go.

You're old enough, I suppose. I'm sure you've kissed plenty of girls already, haven't you?"

Nat's eyes widened as if frightened that Duncan knew something he didn't want him to know.

"You probably have put your arm around her like this," Duncan said, wrapping Nat in his embrace.

He tried shoving Duncan off, but Duncan wouldn't let go.

"And you probably leaned in for a kiss," Duncan went on, putting his face close to Nat's.

"Ew, stop!" Nat said, shoving Duncan harder this time, a smile breaking through his serious face.

"What?" Duncan said with a grin. "You don't wanna kiss me?"

As Duncan approached him, Nat began to run further in front. Though, Duncan went after him, and it soon became a chase. Nat didn't run very far before his brother locked him tight within his arms and smothered his cheeks with wet kisses. All that was heard along the tracks—besides the rustling of the treetops—were the resounding echoes of screaming laughter.

"AND WHERE WILL *YOU* BE STAYING?" Mom asked Duncan as they stood together on their driveway in the early morning. James was there, too. But the sun was still hidden, its light faintly painting the sky.

"There's a little hotel in town," Duncan said. "She'll be at home."

"Okay. Good. Yes. Well, if you want to make it at a reasonable hour."

"Yes, I should go," Duncan told her.

She came up and enveloped herself around him one last time. And it was as if she held him like a child, though Duncan was much taller than she was.

"I tried to get your brother up," she added.

"It's all right. It's summer. I'll be home after the weekend anyway."

Mom's eyes began to glisten, her face reddening.

"It's just the weekend," Duncan repeated.

"Oh, I'm fine," she lied. "Go. Have fun. Say

'hi' to her for me."

"I will."

With that, she turned and walked back toward the garage and into the house.

"I don't know why she does that," James said to Duncan, his hands stuffed in his pockets. "I guess goodbyes are too hard."

"It's just the weekend," Duncan made sure to say a third time.

"It's not *just* the weekend," James said. "Maybe *this* weekend it's just the weekend. But don't kid yourself. It's not just the weekend."

Duncan supposed he was right.

James saw him motion toward the car, so he approached slowly, taking out one of his hands from his pocket. In it was a small black box. He handed it to him.

Duncan didn't have to open it. He knew what it was, but he opened it anyway.

"It was my mother's," James said. "She gave it to me before she passed away. I was going to hold onto it as a keepsake. That's why I didn't give it to *your* mother. But I reckon…might as well."

Duncan didn't know what to say.

"You don't have to give it to her. I'm also not implying you should this weekend. But when the time comes. When both you and Rachel are ready. The Lord will guide you in that."

"…Thank you."

James nodded and gave a humble smile, both hands in his pockets again.

Duncan reached out his hand and waited. James looked surprised at it as if it weren't a hand. For a moment, Duncan thought he might not take it. But he eventually did. James' grip was firm, and Duncan could tell that he was thankful also.

"I don't even know if I want to marry her," Duncan said.

"You don't think so?"

"Well, maybe. But not anytime soon. If so, it'll be years down the road. I want to graduate. Get myself established, you know?"

James chuckled.

"I should go," Duncan told him after some brief silence.

"One moment," James said, grabbing Duncan's arm as he walked toward his car. "I have something else for you."

He took out his wallet from his back pocket.

"James—

"Would you be still for once?"

James unfolded it, retrieved a small, rectangular photo that was placed safely inside, and handed it to him.

The black and white photo was of a boy, probably no more than ten years old. He stood in front of who looked to be his mother and father, out in what seemed to be their front yard, though all that was shown behind them was a dark, ornate door and some brick. They were all squinting because of the sun.

"It's your dad," James said.

The expression on Duncan's face seemed to turn to stone. "Seriously?"

James nodded, smiling. "I know you've been trying to find out more about him. This was all I could find. I'm sorry."

Duncan's eyes drifted back down onto the picture cradled in his hand. He flipped it over, and it was written in calligraphy: *Hosea 6:1*.

1974

THE DAYS FOLLOWING ZACK'S SUDDEN move were grippingly lonesome. Day in and day out, Duncan found himself aimlessly wandering from one place to another, usually somewhere he and Zack would frequent. And those days turned into weeks. And eventually, school came again. The hot air finally dampened, but the sense of isolation was all the more suffocating. The only thing Duncan could manage after school was roaming about near the crick.

So it was not a surprise to him that his dad was able to find him there. He walked up behind his son and tickled his sides. He was granted a smile for a few moments, but Dad noticed Duncan's face again defaulting to a sad state.

"Why so ponderous?" Dad said a bit too lightheartedly as he sat cross-legged beside him, a beer bottle in hand.

"What's *ponderous*?" Duncan asked.

"*Ponderous* is an adjective. It means something like 'heavy' or 'slow'."

"You think I'm fat?"

He smiled. "No. I think you've got a lot on your mind. A heavy thought. Burdensome. It weighs you down. I can see it in your countenance."

"What's *countenance*?"

Dad's smile reinvigorated. "Well…I can tell something's up. That's what I mean. And I know what it is. Your mom and I talk about it quite often. How we see you quite restless. You miss Zack."

"I'm all right," Duncan said, keeping his eyes fixed on the water, since he could not look at his father in the eye with integrity.

"I know. But I also know you're not. I can't

help but think it's partially my fault. I never considered how you would feel. When Zack would leave. And be far away, too. I understand how hard it may be, knowing that you just can't go see him every day. Or really, at all."

"You didn't know what was happening to him," Duncan said despondently. "Or you wouldn't have sent them away."

"Well, about that. Duncan, I'm sorry. I never told you."

Duncan looked up, his heart anxious.

"Well…I called Pastor Dan. That day I said I would. Then he called me back a few days later. He said they never arrived. A week or two passed, and I received a letter from Bill. He said everything was going well. He said the family was well. That everybody was well."

"He's lying!" Duncan shouted, though not meaning to.

"He said he had a sudden, new job opportunity on the other side of Iowa. He didn't say what job. I'm not sure exactly where he's at."

"Can't you just look at the envelope?"

"There was no return address," Dad said. "You

know, Duncan, I don't always feel that I'm making the best choices—for himself or for others…I need you to know that I wouldn't have sent them all that way if I didn't think it was the better option. I knew Pastor Dan was a better counselor than I. And I knew that Bill being here could have worsened. Not simply because of me but because of his own difficult situation here. The choices he'd made. The people he'd gotten involved with. I thought it best for him to start fresh with a trusted pastor I was confident would lead him—better than I could. And Bill seemed all too agreeable. Of course, I hadn't known about the abuse. And I didn't think he'd move elsewhere and not tell me…"

Dad trailed off. Now *he* looked ponderous, taking a long sip of his bottle.

Once he finished, Duncan slowly took it from his hand. There was still a good amount inside. Dad eyed him impatiently.

"How many have you had?" Duncan said.

"…I don't know."

"Is it because you can't remember?"

Duncan noticed Dad's eyes were dark

underneath, his skin a bit clammy.

"Can I have that back?" Dad said, reaching for it.

Duncan's hand that was holding the bottle instinctively backed away from his.

"Duncan. Give it."

Duncan shook his head nervously but with defiance.

Suddenly, Dad swung his hand so fast that the bottle almost flew out of Duncan's hand as he grabbed it. His son's eyes tapered on his father fearfully, his own troubled heartbeat now brought to his awareness.

The glare Dad gave charged with a beast-like power. It only subsided when he broke eye contact to take another drink.

1982

RACHEL LOOKED DUNCAN'S WAY with her hair all done up, her face sparkling with makeup. The dress she wore was pure white and felt like silk. Its train was so long that it curled around her chair.

Duncan looked in her direction. His black blazer was off, hanging sloppily on the back of his own chair. He held her hand delicately, in which one of her fingers sported a silver band and a diamond ring that used to belong to James' mother.

They kissed, and everyone who sat around them applauded. It was a larger wedding than he had anticipated. If it were not for Rachel's side, Duncan would have expected no more than one hundred guests. Nearly three hundred were served.

He and Rachel spent the following hour traveling around the room and speaking to everybody—as many as they could, at least. It was hard because many of them were up and walking about also. The two had only managed to float around four tables before they heard someone at the mic. It was James.

"Can everyone hear me?" He said, his voice amplified. "Good. Well, I hope everyone's enjoying this special occasion. I know it wasn't on the schedule that I'd be up here speaking to all of you. I know the bride and groom are making their rounds right now. So, let me be brief. If you don't know who I am, I'm James Cole. Husband of Sarah Cole. Father of our son, Duncan, who is now himself a husband and—I'm sure—one day soon to be a father as well."

Duncan panned the room awkwardly, wondering who had glanced over his way when they heard that James called him his son. And that's when he saw him—Dad. Duncan's father stood in the back at the open bar, along with a few other fellows Duncan hardly knew. He was chatting lightheartedly with them.

"The Lord is the One who brought these two together," James continued. "It'd only be appropriate to read from God's Word. A psalm, I was thinking. This one was read at our reception. So, I thought it fitting to read it here.

"Rachel. Duncan. I want you both to cling to these words as you go forth in life together. While our Lord has shown great honor to you both today, it is also good to remember—especially when we are most exalted—the humble state we are ever in before Him. Let us take a moment to read Psalm 90."

Darting his eyes back and forth from James to Dad, Duncan anxiously waited for Dad to glance his way.

Lord, you have been our dwelling place
in all generations.
Before the mountains were brought forth,
or ever you had formed the earth and the world,
from everlasting to everlasting you are God.

Dad didn't seem to pay mind to James, nor did he look Duncan's way. He just kept talking with the others. Yet Rachel could see that something was torn within Duncan.

> *You return man to dust and say,*
> *'Return, O children of man!'*
> *For a thousand years in your sight*
> *are but as yesterday when it is past,*
> *or as a watch in the night.*

For a moment, Duncan didn't know what to do. But instinct soon overcame him, and his feet began to shuffle, leaving Rachel with the unfamiliar folks at the table around which they were standing.

> *You sweep them away as with a flood;*
> *they are like a dream,*
> *like grass that is renewed in the morning:*
> *in the morning it flourishes and is renewed;*
> *in the evening it fades and withers*

Those along the perimeter of the banquet hall

were still bustling quietly as James continued to read, allowing Duncan to blend in. He was beginning to be jostled by the thicket of the standing crowd as he neared the bar area. He noticed Dad was finishing up his conversation, giving the other men handshakes.

> *For we are brought to an end by your anger;*
> *by your wrath we are dismayed.*
> *You have set our iniquities before you,*
> *our secret sins in the light of your presence.*

Within a few moments, Dad had begun to walk in the opposite direction—away from Duncan—partially hiding himself within the throng of well-dressed people.

> *For all our days pass away under your wrath;*
> *we bring our years to an end like a sigh.*
> *The years of our life are seventy,*
> *or even by reason of strength eighty;*
> *yet their span is but toil and trouble;*
> *they are soon gone and we fly away.*

Despite Duncan's ever-closer proximity to him, Dad was now well camouflaged within the human brush—lost.

Who considers the power of your anger,
and your wrath according to the fear of you?
So teach us to number our days
that we may get a heart of wisdom.

Duncan's feet stopped, and an internal sigh of disappointment motioned in its place. He was about to amble back to the table where he had left Rachel, but then he saw him again. It was clearly his back. So, Duncan continued into the second large thicket which he was in.

Return, O LORD! How long?
Have pity on your servants!
Satisfy us in the morning with your steadfast love,
that we may rejoice and be glad all our days.

With only a handful of bodies between them, Duncan extended his arm to cut through the remaining few. His hand reached ever forward, finally placing it on Dad's shoulder.

But it wasn't him. At least, it didn't seem so. The man who turned around was much older. His face was marked by years, far more than what would allot a man of Dad's age. Yet, oddly, he resembled him quite exactly had he not appeared as if he were an old man.

Duncan's eyes grew disgustingly wide, his lip quivering slightly. He closed his eyes and opened them again, yet the old man was still there, staring back at him.

The sound of James' voice stopped, a few light claps were given, and within seconds, the room began to bloat with mild chatter.

It seemed as if the old man was about to speak, but fear overtook Duncan, and he backed away, out of the thicket, and back by Rachel's side.

He did not leave her again that night.

1974

IT BECAME MORE DIFFICULT to breathe. The air didn't come as easily, the feeling of death looming larger with every inhale. Then, suddenly, Duncan awoke, finding Nat's head on his stomach. He was still sleeping soundly, using Duncan's body as a pillow.

They were on the couch downstairs. The TV was still playing quietly, but Duncan heard hushed whispers from the other room.

"We need you here," Mom said. It sounded as if she had been crying.

"I *am* here."

"No…You've been gone."

"I'm sorry. I'll stop."

"It's affecting the boys. Me. It's affecting *me*. Your *wife*."

"I'll stop."

"How? As much as I love her, I don't want to be in your mother's place. Having to make the choices she made."

"I *will* stop."

"No. You will get *help*. Or I will get it for you."

"I'll…I'll go somewhere. Lock myself away. I'll clean myself up."

"No. You stay here. We need you *here*. Those boys need a father. And I need my husband."

The conversation stopped momentarily, then Mom continued, "What's gotten into you? Really."

"I don't know where they are," Dad murmured. "I sent them away. And now they're lost, and it's my fault."

Mom sighed. "It's not your fault."

"I should be the one who's lost."

"*Ssshhhh!* Stop that. Don't talk that way."

"It's true."

"This is why you need to stop. You're trying to drink your sorrow away, but it only does the opposite. You know this."

"Sarah—

"I need you to promise me. Like you did years ago. That you would take care of us. And part of that means taking care of yourself. I can help you, but I can't do it *for* you."

After a moment, she said again, "Promise me."

"…Okay," Dad said weakly.

1985

ITS EYES WERE AS BLACK AS COAL, staring at him. Duncan sat frozen, unable to move, though wanting to. It was only when he heard the sound of a gunshot and a murderous scream that he finally jolted awake.

Duncan was sweating, though it was cold. Frost clung to the windows. At least Rachel was beside him to help keep warm.

A moment passed before the distant sound of whining entered his ears. He felt Rachel begin to move, but he gently brought his hands to her shoulders until she lay still. Duncan placed his bare feet on the hard floor and crept to the other room where the baby was whining.

The moonlight hung perfectly over his cradle, revealing his tiny scrunched-up face. Tears were mercilessly pouring down. And without thought, Duncan scooped him up in his hands and brought him to his chest. His legs instinctively began to bob, creating a rocking motion.

The baby cried for some time. But after a while, his crying ebbed away into a coo and then silence.

"There you go, Patrick," Duncan whispered softly in his ear. "You all better now?"

The baby must have felt some comfort, since his eyes began to close dreamfully, and Duncan could feel his breathing settle.

1987

"GO AHEAD. DO THE HONORS," said James.

And so Duncan went over to the *for sale* sign and used much of his strength to fork it out of the ground.

"Didn't think it'd be that difficult," Duncan said with a laugh.

Rachel bent down and picked up a mallet from the ground. "Perhaps that was intentional," she said to Duncan.

After removing the signage and placing it in the garage, they walked to the backyard—all four of them—except for Patrick, who was being carried by Mom. Though the homes were nestled close together on either side, the yard extended for miles, it seemed.

"It goes on for nearly two acres," said James. "But you know all this."

"I will admit," Duncan told him, "you found us a good deal."

"I said having a realtor in the family will come in handy. Now," Mom said, directing her comment to James, "it's time to find *us* a good deal."

"You're moving?" Duncan said a bit too abrasively.

"Probably not," she said. "We'd like to."

"Why?"

"Well, you boys are out of the house now. Nat just got married. It's too big of a home for just James and I. And we live so far away from you."

James sighed. "One day," he said as he wrapped one of his arms around Mom.

Her hair was thinning again like it had at one point years ago. The sides of her face appeared more sunken in than the last time they had come to visit. And her arms seemed to have elongated—

they looked so frail.

"One day soon," she said, beaming up at him.

1990

"LIKE THIS," Duncan said to Patrick.

They were on the back deck, Duncan on his knees with a paint roller in hand.

"It looks sticky," Patrick said, gaping at his dad.

Rachel was on the other end of the deck with a roller in her hand, as well.

"Listen to your father," she said as she kept painting.

"It's only sticky if you let it dry on you," Duncan told him. "Watch me. You take the roller, and you roll it gently in the pan. Let the paint get all over it, you see? Then, you firmly but carefully rub it along the board. Like this. You want to paint in the same direction as the boards. Lengthwise. Simple, right? Here. Now you try."

"But I don't want—

"'Yes, sir,'" Rachel inserted for Patrick to repeat.

He did so with a sigh. "Yes, sir."

Patrick, with pursed lips, reached for the roller in Duncan's hand. But before he could grab it, Duncan put the roller on his son's shirt and started to paint on *him*.

"Hey!" Patrick exclaimed.

Rachel turned around and began to laugh.

"Mommy!"

"Here, let me help you," she said, grinning.

Rachel brought her paint roller over and, to Patrick's shock, began to paint him, too.

"Hey!" he gasped, though giggling this time.

Duncan put his roller down and placed his hands in the paint-filled pan. Then, he rubbed Patrick's cheeks and arms with them.

They lost a good amount of paint that afternoon. Duncan had to run to the store the next day, but he was quite certain the memory would outlast what they were putting on the deck boards.

1992

DUNCAN'S EYES FLOATED UP from the papers on his desk to the clock on the wall. It was well past nine o'clock. He removed his reading glasses and rubbed the bridge of his nose, breathing in deeply.

That was it. He was done. Duncan organized the papers and gathered them into a folder, which he kept in a drawer underneath. He flicked off the warm-lit lamp, exited the room, and shut the study door behind him. He paused, straining to hear some sound of life. As he crept down the hall, he found Patrick asleep on the couch. The book his son was reading still lay open in his hand, so

Duncan went over and slowly slipped it out of his grasp and onto the coffee table.

Though his eyes were shut, Patrick knew what his dad was about to do. He extended his arms upward so that his dad could pick him up. Duncan walked lightly on the hardwood floor. Rachel was at the table as he cut through the kitchen, writing in her journal under one lit candle.

"You know there's electricity in this house," Duncan whispered to her.

"Oh, I forgot," she said. "All this time, and I've been wasting all this wax…Patrick's gone, it looks like."

"Yeah."

Rachel shut her book and followed them to his bedroom. Duncan placed him under the covers tenderly and was about to shut the door behind him when she crawled up to his bedside and sat on the floor next to him. She brushed his hair as she began to sing softly the same old, familiar tune.

Close your eyes to this world of sin and sorrow
Not in fear for what may come tomorrow

But in wait for Him who finds those sleeping
That He may wake you while in fretful dreaming
For Christ alone can open up your eyes
Only He can from slumber make your rise
So when the light of day surely breaks again
You would see His face, your true and faithful Friend

When she finished her song, Rachel kissed him and quietly stood up. Duncan waited for her under the doorframe.

"What," she said as she walked into the hall again.

Duncan kept staring at her, beaming.

"Quit it," she said as she past him, blushing down the hall.

Duncan followed her, and before she ultimately got away, he took her hand and wouldn't let go. She turned to look at him, her eyes longing for his embrace.

He pulled her in and held her there in the faint light. They swayed back and forth as if romantic music surrounded them, though it was so quiet that they could hear the creaking of the floorboards under them.

Duncan's face pressed on her longingly. He held her close. His lips met her hair, which then traveled down to her lips and further still.

Rachel took his hand and placed it on her stomach. For a moment, he kept on kissing her. Then, he noticed she wanted him to pause and look at her, so he did.

With his hand still placed over her navel and her bright green eyes unhinged, Duncan finally understood. No words were needed.

She was pregnant.

1974

DUNCAN AND HIS MOM SAT on the floor across from one another at the coffee table in the living room. A chessboard lay between them. It was her turn.

She looked intently at the pieces. A knight was blocking her king from moving in the only place it could go, and she noticed Duncan's rook was about to ride up the board. She knew what that meant.

"Well, I think you've got me," she said, resigning herself to defeat.

"No I haven't. Look over here."

Duncan slid her black bishop across the board, creating a barrier between the king and his soon-approaching rook.

"Yeah, I think you'll be ready for chess club this year," she said, smiling. "You don't need me to help you practice anymore."

"Come on, don't give up."

"Honey, this is the third game I've played you tonight."

The front door suddenly opened. It was Dad with Nat on his shoulders.

"Duck your head," he said to Nat. "All right, get your PJs on. Quick."

Dad set him down speedily and popped his butt as Nat skidded across the room and flung himself up the stairs with the help of the banister.

Dad plopped into his recliner as if he had just come in from doing something laborious.

"Duncan. Can you get me a glass of water?" he said.

Duncan sped his rook to the back of the board, moved Mom's only pawn that could do something, grabbed her bishop with his rook, and called out "checkmate" before standing up and rushing into the kitchen.

Nat soon thundered down the stairs as Duncan appeared from the kitchen with Dad's water. Nat purposely fell on Mom, who was now spread out on the couch.

"Thanks, Son," Dad said to him, taking one long gulp.

Duncan went to the cupboard without thought and retrieved four blue hymnals.

"I'll share with Nat. Thank you, Honey."

"All right," said Dad, his Bible flopped over his large armrest. Duncan sat on the floor beside him.

"Let's pray first," Dad continued. "Who are we going to pray for tonight?"

"We're going to keep praying for the Burns family," Mom answered. "For Bill, and Karen, and Zack."

Dad and his son met eyes for a moment before intentionally shifting elsewhere.

"And for the boys' first week of school," Dad added.

"And for more time together," Nat tagged on, making everyone smile, though Dad's faded first.

1993

RACHEL HAD HER HANDS CLASPED over Duncan's eyes despite the room being pretty dark as it was. Patrick had just turned off all the kitchen lights except for the one above the sink.

Duncan could feel her chuckling to herself by the way her hands shook slightly.

"What?" Duncan said.

"Okay, open," Mom called out.

When he opened them, a six-layer carrot cake with thick cream cheese frosting lay before him at the table. It was leaning slightly to its side, but it was determined to stand. The whole thing looked a bit unstable as an army of lit candles braved the top.

"How many are on here?" asked Duncan with casual amazement.

"Thirty," James said. "You know why?"

"I wonder…"

"Well," Rachel interjected. "Blow it out."

"Aren't you all going to sing?" Duncan said.

"Don't you see the cake? Save us first. Then we'll praise you."

Duncan gave Rachel a sarcastic look before inhaling deeply, similar to the waves that go out to sea before a tsunami bursts forth.

LATER THAT EVENING, after everyone had their fill of the six-layered leaning cake, they brought Duncan into the living room. Rachel gasped slightly as she sat down on the sofa with him.

"Are you all right?" he asked her.

"Yeah."

"You are well overdue, after all," Mom said. "You could pop at any moment."

Rachel's stomach was incredibly bloated, and

Duncan wondered if there might have been twins in there.

"I don't think Duncan would want to share his birthday," Rachel joked.

Patrick came up to Rachel and tried to sit on her lap, but James whistled and opened his arms, signaling that it'd be wise to let his mama be right now.

"Well," Rachel said after a longer pause than she was comfortable with. "Enough about me. Here. Duncan. Open this."

She mustered her strength, hauled a box from the floor that was more swollen than she was, and had it land awkwardly in Duncan's lap

"Hey, Patrick," he said. "Come here."

His son knew what that meant, bouncing off James' lap and running straight toward him.

"I'm needing some help."

And without any time to spare, Patrick ripped off the wrapping paper. It was a stovetop grille.

"So you can feel like a man even in the winter," she said.

"Ha...Bit jeering tonight, I see," Duncan commented with a reassuring smile.

"I'm pregnant," she reminded him.

"I can vouch for her," Mom added. "When I was pregnant with you, Honey, I said things I'd never say otherwise. The same thing happened when I had your brother."

"Okay, my turn," James said, standing up from where he was and walking to the foyer closet.

He opened it, and there lay another present hidden amongst the scattered shoes. That, too, was seemingly heavy, as James' cherry red face indicated when he lugged it over to Duncan.

"You know what to do," Duncan commanded Patrick.

And he did a great job, leaving no tape stuck to the sides. It was a toolset.

"So you can stop 'borrowing' mine," James said, using air quotes. "How long have you two been married and haven't had your own set?"

"You're the one who insisted I used yours," Duncan replied.

"Well, now I insist you have your own. So here."

"Well, thank you."

Mom began to chuckle to herself. "You know,

Honey," she said to James as he sat back down on the piano bench with her, "I can't help but think how, when you were a kid, you stashed your father's tools in the landscaping out here, so you wouldn't have to help him work. Believe it or not, I found one deep inside the bush as I helped Rachel clear up the fallen leaves the other day. I bet it's your father's."

"Wait, what?" Duncan interjected, confused.

Mom's eyes widened briefly before returning to normal—too normal. James looked at her like she had said something she shouldn't have. And maybe she really shouldn't have.

"You lived here?" Duncan asked James.

He sighed.

"You lived here, and you never thought to mention it to me?" said Duncan.

"Honey, it's not like that."

Duncan paused for a moment, a flood of thoughts rushing in, like pieces of a puzzle that somehow managed to come together on its own.

"I don't know," Duncan replied. "If it wasn't a big deal, he wouldn't have hid it. James would have told me, wouldn't you?"

"Duncan," James began, "I'm sorry I didn't say anything."

Duncan looked at him, his eyes furrowing, his teeth clenching, his heart pumping. He had to stand up.

"Honey, sit down."

"Who's life is this?" Duncan said in a low, hushed tone, still directing his words at James. "Mine? This isn't my house. It's yours. You said you found it at a good deal, but I bet you owned this house all along and sold it to me for cheap."

"So what if he did?" Mom inserted. "What's the harm in that?"

Duncan ignored her. "And you never mentioned to tell me that you went to the same college. The college you encouraged me to apply to. And went. The college *you* attended."

"I didn't know you knew," James admitted.

"You thought in those four years, I wouldn't have found out?"

"You said you wanted to know more about your father," James informed me. "And that's the college *he* went to."

"Yet you couldn't have said that you went

there, too? How simple that would've been."

"Perhaps you wouldn't have gone," Mom added weakly.

"So that's it," Duncan said, still to James. "You kept all these secrets so I could walk in *your* footsteps. You knew that if I knew, I wouldn't be fooled. This whole time, I've just been a passive pawn bending to your will. I don't understand. Is this really *my* life? Is this really my son? Is she my wife? Or is she your daughter?"

"Duncan!" said Mom, her voice raised now.

Silence engulfed the entire scene. Rachel's gaze ducked under the coffee table. James' darted around the room. Patrick couldn't lay his off his father.

Duncan resigned to the closet and grabbed his jacket.

"Duncan," Mom pleaded. "James, say something."

But he remained silent. No words ushered Duncan's way as he grabbed the keys that hung on the wall by the entrance window. "I'll be back," he said unconvincingly.

The only sound that echoed back from the

heavy stillness was the shutting of the front door.

Duncan wasn't sure at first where he was driving to. Fury fueled the way. But soon, the green numbers on the dash quickly ticked on by. One hour passed into two. Eventually, he found himself on the same street where the old, white-clad church building stood. He was home.

He turned into the parking lot, where one single light cast an extremely orange glow. The church building loomed larger in front of the windshield as he parked by its entrance.

But Duncan didn't go inside, despite Dad's old key to the building hanging on his keychain. No. Instead, he used a flashlight that he kept in one of the door pockets and walked through the woods, over the now-precarious wooden bridge, and out onto his old backyard. Though he didn't have a key to their house on his chain, Duncan did know where to find it.

His hand hovered over the river rocks that landscaped the home until he felt one a bit unlike the others. He seized it and turned it over, where a hidden opening on the backside was found, providing a spare key into the house.

The first thing Duncan noticed when he opened the back kitchen door was the analog clock on the wall in front of him, lit only by the moon. It was well past ten.

Though, almost immediately after, he became aware of some distant sound. A voice. Creeping in cautiously, he scanned the darkness.

By its animatronic quality, Duncan understood it to come from the answering machine.

…So pray. And come.

The answering machine gave a high-pitched sound, indicating the person had just hung up. Without delay, Duncan went over to the telephone and saw a button flashing near it. A missed call.

He pressed the button.

Duncan, it's James. Look, we're not sure where you went. I thought maybe you drove to our house. So I'm calling. I guess you're not there…But maybe you are. Rachel's in labor. We're all at the hospital, but she's having some complications.

I'm not sure if you'll be able to call back, and I know it's late, but it might be wise to come as soon as possible. I know there's nothing you can do, humanly speaking, but you should be here. We'll be here, so don't speed. There's nothing you can do at this point but pray. So pray. And come.

The furnace kicked on right as the message ended. Duncan stood there in the blackness, shivering—but not because of the cold.

MOM AND PATRICK WERE IN SIGHT. He had his head on her lap, his eyes hidden behind his eyelids. It was nearly three in the morning.

James kept pacing slowly about the waiting area, even when he saw Duncan, making sure not to meet his gaze.

Duncan went over to Mom. She had tears in her eyes.

"Hey, Sweetie," she smiled feebly.

Her eyes were incredibly red, though Duncan wasn't sure if the late hour was the cause. They wouldn't let go of him.

"What is it, Mom?" Duncan said softly. "Where's Rachel?"

More tears welled up along the bottom row of

her eyelashes.

She finally ripped her eyes off him and onto James.

And so James turned around to face Duncan. He kept himself in the corner, a distance away. He appeared to be examining the blue carpeting, his hands tucked in his pockets.

"There was…a lot of blood," he said.

Now Duncan's eyes were welling up.

"Duncan, I'm so sorry…" James added, trailing off, almost unable to get the last of it out.

Duncan's head instinctively nodded, his lip quivering involuntarily. It took a good long moment to gather himself, at least enough to speak.

"…And the baby?"

At first, no response. But then, James said, almost in a whisper, "She's in the back with the nurses…waiting for you."

A few long, drawn-out breaths were taken before Duncan found any stability. When he regained a sense of movement eventually, he glanced at the attendant at the desk, who unlocked the large door for him, and he left the three of them.

"Right this way, Mr. McLaughlin," a nurse at the end of the hall called politely.

Duncan followed her, though at a distance, around a few bends and down a few corridors, when at last she opened a door and held it for him.

Duncan entered. Another nurse was there, rocking as she stood, her back toward him. Soon, however, she turned around, and in her arms was his baby girl. Without a word, the nurse who held his daughter brought her over to him and placed her in his care.

The heartbeat of the baby pulsed on Duncan's skin. Despite her little eyes being closed, she reached out her hand, waiting to hold onto something. So he slowly craned his neck forward and placed his cheek where her tiny hand was, allowing her to feel his face, though wet as it was.

1974

IT WAS WHAT ZACK HAD FEARED. His window looked out onto an endless crop, into the haze, as if heaven were only a stretch of thick clouds.

He peered out from it many times over the few months he'd been there, imagining lines on the windows resembling bars.

Today was different. He hadn't glanced out once. His eyes stuck to the ceiling as he lay in bed, determined to stay there. He didn't even toss his baseball in the air like he usually would on these dull occasions.

From the static silence, a voice resounded

from afar, beyond the closed bedroom door, and further still.

"Zack!" his mother beckoned. "Mail's here."

He sighed a dreary breath before picking himself up onto his feet and out of his room.

"Here," she said as he came slumping into the kitchen.

Zack reached for the stack of envelopes, but she grabbed his shoulder and brought him close.

"Let me see," she said.

She tucked her hand around his chin and raised his head. A plum-colored mark bruised his cheekbone.

"It's better," his mother said. "After you look through these, I'll get my makeup bag so we can fix you up before we go out for dinner."

"I don't want to go out," he said flatly.

"It's your birthday."

"I don't want to go out."

"Well, what do *you* want? We'll do what you want. I'll tell Daddy. He'll...I'm sure he'll be fine, whatever you choose."

"I want to go home."

"Sweetheart..." she trailed off for a moment.

"Daddy's trying to find a job. But then we'll move. Probably somewhere closer into town. Maybe around Christmas. That's only three months away."

"I want to go home," Zack repeated.

She sighed. "I know—

"Without him."

His mother's eyes gave away her sudden fright as the two looked at each other.

"It's possible," Zack continued. "You know what he's doing."

"No, sweetheart. We've already discussed—

"Please."

"…We can't."

"Dad's not even home." Zack softened his voice as if someone else were there. "No one's stopping us."

Her eyes dropped slightly, tired.

"Not today," she whispered wearily. "Let's not talk about this today."

Zack knew it was useless.

"You know what?" she said, handing the stack of envelopes to him, then standing as tall as she could, her voice a bit too optimistic. "I'm going to go into town, and I'm going to pick up a big cake. A chocolate cake. Your favorite. And some balloons. And that frozen lasagna you really enjoyed last time."

Zack was too deflated to respond.

He stood there as she kissed him on the forehead, grabbed her purse, and scooted out the door without another word. He thought he saw her beginning to cry as she exited, though he was unsure.

Zack crept up to the window slowly, where the translucent curtains were drawn. He waited a minute after the car had exited the driveway and out of sight, among the corn.

His hand still had the mail in his hand as his eyes seemed to remain unhinged at the windowsill.

Then he left. He placed the mail neatly on the dining table before putting on his worn shoes and grabbing the rust-bitten bike that leaned against the side of the garage.

The sun hung low for some time as he sped down the poorly-paved backroads of the Iowan countryside. A snake slithered across one of the streets Zack was going down, which he managed to pass without difficulty, though he looked back as he kept peddling, as if to think the snake would chase after him.

He'd finally put his hand on the handlebar breaks as he went off the road and into the tall grass that went up the train tracks. Zack biked alongside it for a bit until he began to hear the faintest cry of a siren. A train was coming.

The sun finally hid itself behind the blackened trees, causing a hint of soft orange to line the horizon, as he hid the bike among the grass and stepped over the rail and onto the planks. Zack shuffled toward the siren, his hands in his pockets, staring far into the distance. At first, he couldn't see it. Then, a bright beam emerged from the black thicket and quickly showed right on him.

The siren grew louder. The tracks rumbled more thunderously. Zack didn't move except to remove one of his hands from his pocket—the one with the scar sliced across his palm. He examined it, attempting to focus on the moment he got it. But a greater thought overwhelmed him. In fear, his head darted upward toward the blinding light as the hypnotic whistle now screamed.

*   *   *

THE SCHOOL BUS SQUEALED TO A HALT, letting Nat and Duncan off at the stop sign that stood just beyond the train tracks. The day was bright, causing Duncan to shift his ball cap downward to cover a good portion of his face in order and keep from squinting.

"Hey! That's our house!" Nat said in excitement, pointing at the ninth one away. "Let's race!"

"No, I'm good—

"Go!" he shouted anyway, his feet already on the move.

Duncan reluctantly picked up his own with a bit more haste, eventually getting into a steady run. He did not attempt to compete against his seven-year-old brother—not until the last few houses. Then, Duncan's legs stretched further out with each step, passing him quickly.

He caught his breath as he stood there on their driveway, waiting for Nat.

"That's not fair," Nat whined as he finally stepped into their yard.

"You said you wanted to race," Duncan told him, still panting a little.

"I get a head start next time," he said as he crossed the grass, his face pouting.

Duncan caught up to him by the time they reached the front door, messing up his hair with his hand.

"I'm gonna get the chessboard," Nat said hopefully.

"Sure. It's in my room."

Nat opened the door and sped quickly up the steps without setting down his backpack first.

"…Once he knew, she said he left. That was three days ago," Duncan heard his mom say in the other room.

Then, suddenly, all Duncan could hear was Nat rummaging through his room upstairs.

Duncan slumped his bag by the door and ambled through the living room and into the kitchen, where he found Dad holding Mom's hand delicately as she leaned back against the counter. Her other hand was holding a crumpled-up tissue.

Her face was covered up by the hanging cabinets. Still, as Duncan made his way over to meet them, it was revealed that the area around her eyes was very red, as well as her nose. Dad's expression was grim.

No one knew who should speak first.

"Hey, Honey," said Mom defeatedly.

"What's the matter?" Duncan asked, trying not to sound too concerned.

"It's about Zack," Dad said in her place.

"What about Zack?" he asked. "You know where he's at?"

Mom's face scrunched up, her hand quickly raised to meet her face and wipe her eyes with the overused tissue.

"Karen finally called," he said. "They were near Davenport. That's clear on the other side of where Pastor Dan lives."

"*Were*? They moved?"

Mom looked as if she was about to burst.

"Honey. Zack…" But she couldn't go on.

She didn't have to, though. The foreboding atmosphere seemed to give it away.

The scene began to crystalize from Duncan's sight. He could tell his face wanted to turn into the same state as Mom's.

"Duncan," Dad said softly as he let go of Mom's hand and approached his son.

"Don't," Duncan said firmly, backing up.

But Dad kept crawling up slowly. So Duncan bolted—out the door and across the yard, into the woods. At first, he thought he was running alone, but then he heard cracks of twigs and leaves behind him. Soon enough, a large hand grabbed Duncan's arm and spun him around.

Dad bent down to meet him. Duncan's hands tried to shove him away, but he was too strong. He continued to struggle as Dad brought him close.

"Get—off!" Duncan yelled, locking his arms against his chest. But it was no use. Dad pulled him in tightly, wrapping his arms around him firmly. Though, Duncan kept squirming, hoping for release.

"*Stop*," Dad pleaded in a gentle whisper, "Stop. Stop."

After a minute had lapsed, Duncan finally gave up. The muscles in his body relaxed, and he wept on his dad's shoulder until he soaked a portion of his shirt.

1998

PATRICK'S DOOR SWUNG OPEN without care. He lay there in his bed, his hair long and disheveled, his head buried in his pillow.

"Patrick!" Duncan said. "This is the last time I'm telling you. You have five minutes. Let's go!"

With that, he shut the door behind him just as carelessly.

The next door that was opened was Ruth's. Duncan quietly snuck up to her bed. She was still asleep, too, but he did not use the same tactic on her as his son. Instead, Duncan stroked her hair and kissed it.

"Happy Birthday, Sweetheart," he whispered with a smile.

Ruth raised her arms though her eyes were still shut. Duncan scooped her up as if she were still two years old—but not without a mild grunt.

"Getting so big," he said.

They went over to the kitchen together, though no surprise awaited her. Duncan placed her on a chair with two pillows so her arms could easily reach over the table.

Nearly ten minutes passed before Duncan heard a pair of feet slumping down the hall. At least it gave him time to make his lunch.

"Patrick, what are you wearing?" Duncan said as he caught a glimpse of him trodding into the kitchen.

He looked down at it lazily. "…Clothes."

"You wore those yesterday. And it was gym day, too. Go back and change, please."

Patrick turned around slackly and headed for his room again—but not without first putting his hand in Ruth's cereal so as to grab a few puffs, causing the milk to splatter everywhere.

"*Heeeyy!*" Ruth shouted.

Duncan had turned away for one moment to finish the sandwich, and when he looked back, it appeared as if the cereal had had a minor explosion.

"Hey! Get back over here. Get a wet rag and clean that up."

"I thought you said to go and change."

"Yeah, your attitude. About your clothes, I guess you're just gonna have to stink. You know, tell your friends you can't manage yourself. I'm sure that'll at least appreciate your honesty."

Duncan pretended not to notice his eye roll and went back to fixing the rest of his lunch. Meanwhile, Patrick headed over to the sink to fetch a rag. He damped it under the faucet, but as he did so, something outside captured his attention.

"Hey, Dad?"

Duncan turned around to face him.

"The bus just passed," Patrick said.

All Duncan could manage was a sigh.

* * *

DUNCAN STOPPED THE CAR near the middle school entrance.

"Did you grab your lunch?" he asked Patrick through the rearview mirror.

Sorry was all his son said as he unbuckled himself and opened the door onto the sidewalk, forcing the cool air to gust into the vehicle and make Ruth shiver.

"Hey…I love you."

But Patrick shut the door abrasively and huffed away.

Duncan stretched over the car and rolled down his passenger window. "Patrick!"

His son turned around, noticing Duncan was waiting for him to come back. He did so stiffly.

"I know it's a hard day," Duncan said when he finally came close enough for him to speak normally. "It is for *all* of us. You know that."

"Can I go now?"

"Your mother would want you to have a good day at school."

Patrick glanced at Ruth through the backseat window coldly. "If it wasn't for *her*, she'd still be here."

"*Patrick!*"

He quickly turned around once more to face the school building.

"PATRICK!" Duncan yelled again as he walked away, ignoring him.

DUNCAN'S FEET SOFTLY MOTIONED ACROSS the wooden floor, the light spilling into the hallway from the different open rooms—except for Ruth's.

He rapped on the door before letting himself in. "Ruthie?"

He poked his head around the door to find her curled up underneath her comforter. She looked glum.

He opened the door all the way and stood underneath the doorframe. "Still thinking about what Patrick said?" Duncan asked.

She nodded, so he went over and sat beside her on the bed, caressing her hair with his fingers. Her face was wet from tears, so he took a part of his shirt and wiped them away.

"There you go," he said. "All better."

They looked at each other, Duncan trying to

give a reassuring expression. "Did Patrick happen to apologize to you at all?"

She nodded.

"Well, that's good, at least," he said.

"Did I really make Mama die?"

"No, of course not...Patrick—he's just angry. He misses her and doesn't know what to do about it."

"Why's he angry at *me*?"

Duncan looked at her for a moment, trying to find the right words to respond with. "Because she died the same day you were born. You've known that."

"So I did make Mama die?"

"No," he said again, this time more firmly. "There's no one to blame."

"What'd she look like?"

"You know what she looks like, Ruthie. We have pictures all around the house."

"I know," she said. "I just like it when you tell it."

Smiling, Duncan said, "Well...all you'd have to do is look in the mirror. You have her eyes. Those beautiful green eyes. And your hair, so curly and brown. Just like hers."

"Just like hers?"

"Just like hers."

She giggled. Then, she said, "Is she with Jesus?"

"…Yes."

"How do you know?"

"Well, she was really loved by Jesus. Jesus loved her so much that He wanted her to be with Him forever. That's even why He died for her."

"Is that why He took her? Because He didn't want to be without her anymore?"

"No. Jesus was with her even when she was here. And she believed that He loved her."

"So why'd he take her?"

"Well," said Duncan, "we're all taken at some point. Some people are taken when they're old. Some when they're young. I don't know why Jesus took her so soon. Maybe He'll tell me one day. When I'm with Him, too."

"Tell Jesus not to take you too soon, okay, Daddy?"

Duncan raised a weak smile. "I can ask."

* * *

IT DAWNED ON DUNCAN that the house was unusually quiet. He was finishing the last fold of laundry at the kitchen table—the windows that led outside were now pitch—and he glanced over at the oven to discover the clock reveals that it was well over nine o'clock.

Duncan stood up from the chair and stretched a little, grunting as he took the first few steps. In the other room, Patrick was asleep on the couch. For a moment, Duncan remained where he was, watching his son breathe peacefully. But then Duncan decided to gather him in his arms— which was far more difficult these days—and carried him to his room. He knelt by his bed and laid him under his covers. There, he softly sang to him Rachel's lullaby.

THE DAYS GREW COLDER to the point of blistering, and the leaves now blanketed the ground. Ruth was helping Patrick rake the back while Duncan started on the front. People passed along the sidewalk in their scarves and flannels as he worked—old couples, young couples, couples with dogs, couples with children. After a while, Duncan didn't feel like raking anymore.

Instead, he sat on the front porch step, cupped his hands, and prayed. And after he prayed for a while, he took out his wallet that he always kept in the back pocket of his jeans and took out a few small photographs that were inside. The one on top was of Rachel. She was in her wedding dress. He wasn't in it, but she looked happy as she sat at the table. It appeared as if she was about to fall off her chair.

And then there was that old photo James had given him years ago—of Dad as a kid. He examined it as he sometimes still would.

"Still trying to figure it out?" said a voice, a soothing voice. A voice he recognized.

Duncan's eyes shifted from the photo upward. Rachel was standing in front of him, many feet apart, on the front sidewalk leading up to the porch.

"I told you to let me know what you find out," she said.

Duncan wasn't too surprised that she was there. "I told you all I knew."

"Oh, come on," she grinned. "You know more than you want to believe. That's the truth, isn't it?"

"I'm sorry, who are we talking about?"

"You know, Duncan. I think you knew all these years and didn't want to tell me."

"Didn't want to tell you what?"

She sighed. "Well. If you won't say, I guess I'll just go—

"Wait—where are you going?"

"I can't tell you that. That wouldn't be fair."

"Rachel. What are you doing?"

"What?"

"…Aren't you gonna stay?"

"Stay?" she said.

"Stay with me. Our kids would want to see you. You can't just go."

"That's not how it works."

"Stop being so cryptic," Duncan said with a laugh, though there was nothing funny about this conversation.

Without another word, Rachel's smile widened, her eyes squinting, and she turned from

Duncan, ambling toward the road.

"Rachel!" Duncan called to her.

But she kept walking. Out onto the street. Then, onto the neighbor's yard. For a moment, he wasn't sure what she would do. Then, she knocked on the door, and it opened. Rachel went inside without a backward glance.

He sat on the porch step for a moment more, quite frustrated at what just transpired. But once he looked down at the photo again, Duncan noticed something. In the background was a dark and ornate door—the same door that seemed to embellish the ramshackle of a house across the road.

His body rose from where it was, now bracing himself for what he was about to do. His feet stepped down onto the sidewalk, crossed the road, and marched onto the other side—like Rachel had done.

Duncan hesitated. His hand was only a few inches from the door, ready to knock on it, when something stopped him. Fear, perhaps. Or maybe it was the unwillingness to know what truths may emerge from the other side.

He brandished the door anyway, and within moments, someone who looked to be his father stood underneath its frame. But it wasn't him. He was older. The wrinkles on his face were etched like scars, his hair a salty color.

"Are you—

"Don't you get sentimental with me," the old man stopped him.

"Sorry, I don't really know who you are," Duncan told him.

"Really? I don't buy that for a second."

The man kept the door open but walked back inside his home.

"Have you been stalking me?" Duncan asked, standing right where I was.

"You were the one who bought that house across the street. From *me*. I think you got it backwards…Comin' in or not?"

For a moment, Duncan paused, surveying him. But eventually, he walked through the threshold. Immediately, Duncan noticed what smelled worse than moth balls—mold. And there was a lot of junk that he needed to maneuver around. Beer bottles lay everywhere, some broken.

The walls worn. Haven't been repapered in forty years or so, if Duncan had to guess.

The kitchen was no different. Piles of disheveled newspapers were stacked listlessly on the table, the medicine strewn around them.

The old man strolled over to one of his dingy cabinets and retrieved two shot glasses.

"You were at my wedding," Duncan said, his recall finally pushing through.

"Ain't that what an invite's for?"

"I didn't invite you. It must have been my mother."

"No," he said. "That stiff man she's with invited me."

"James? He doesn't even know you."

"Doesn't know me?" the old man said with a dark laugh. "I've known him since he was a tyke."

The man took the glasses and went over to another cabinet, where he clunked them down carelessly on the counter and reached for a liquor bottle.

"You're my dad's father. Aren't you?"

The old man halted his pouring and turned back to Duncan.

"Look at you," the old man said. "No respect. Won't even call me your grandfather."

"I mean, you weren't a father to *my* father," Duncan said back.

The old man's face turned a sour expression. He finished his pouring, drank his shot, and shattered it on the ground recklessly.

"You're the reason my father was a drunk," Duncan added.

"No," he replied, stopping him. "Your father made his own choices."

"It mustn't have helped that his own father encouraged him to drink at such a young age. That's why he left. Because of *you.*"

The man's eyes floated downward.

"Why you here?" the man said, refusing to look up again. "Lived here long enough. Never came to say hello."

"You must have never left the house. I've never seen you."

"So why you here? Thinkin' he's hidin' in this house a mine? Go ahead. Tear up them floorboards if you want. Ain't even no ghost livin' here."

"I don't know why I knocked," Duncan admitted. "Maybe I did think I'd see him. At least a piece of him, anyway."

The old man's eyes flicked up at Duncan's last statement before hovering back down again.

"I want you gone," the old man said, though quietly, as if to himself.

"Listen. I know it ended badly between you two. But I don't think it has to be that way."

"What you talkin' 'bout? Wasn't you the one to see it happen, anyhow? Yet you comin' to me sayin' things that ain't possible."

"All I'm saying—

"I said I want you gone," he demanded.

Duncan sighed long and heavy, tempted to speak one more thing before removing himself from the situation. But in the end, he simply walked out without another word.

DUNCAN'S HAIR WAS STILL QUITE DAMP as he exited the bathroom. A single lamp on his bedside dresser lit his bedroom dimly, which was where Duncan headed. He examined the framed photos that lay spread out across it before opening the bottom drawer and fetching a t-shirt to wear.

The top drawer was cracked open, though, which he thought was strange. He opened it, finding Rachel's clothes still neatly folded inside, as it had been all these years. Her journals lay stacked off to the side.

The black leather felt soft and worn on his fingers as Duncan picked one up in his hands. Albeit, its binding was a bit stiff when he opened its pages.

There, he saw written on the first page:

Rachel Jordan Rose's
Psalms, Poems & Prayers
September 1977 — June 1978

Duncan sat on his bed while he slowly turned the aged pages. But his finger stopped on one that he remembered. Rachel had read it to him when they were in college.

There she lay atop the muck, Duncan began to read. A felt grief slowly froze his body as he made his way down to the last line, *The Father's love will bring her home.*

"Duncan?" he heard from down the hallway.

It was Rachel. Or maybe it was just one of the kids. Duncan went over and peered out the door. The hallway was almost unrecognizably dark, with both Patrick's and Ruth's doors shut for the night. However, Duncan continued to hear something—the faint sound of what seemed to be a fixed, high-pitched beep—emanating from the living room.

Slowly, he crept down the corridor and noticed a dim light was on as he emerged into the room. And something else, too. The moment Duncan scanned the room, he found a gurney with a body and a sheet covered over it. It was hooked up to a heart monitor, but right when he had entered the room, the high-pitched beep went flat.

His feet refused to move any further, but something about this scene gave him chills. Duncan shut his eyes for a second to garner some resolve within himself, then he went up to the gurney carefully. His hand reached for the sheet and began to pull on it when he stopped. He could feel his heart racing, his arms quivering. But as steadily as he could, Duncan continued to pull down the sheet. It was Rachel. Her skin was awfully pale, her eyes shut, her cheeks sunken in a little. She was dead.

Anger swept over him unexpectedly, and he tore the rest of the sheet off. She was nothing but skin and bones. The unsightly image forced Duncan backward, and he fell.

Soon, he heard a whistle rise, overtaking the sound of the monitor. It was as if it came from a train that was plowing at full speed down the road. So Duncan got up on his feet and rushed to the door. When he opened it, he found a body strewn in the middle of the street. Without hesitation, he hurried over to it, but as he stepped closer, it became clearer that the body was Zack's. And he was not alone. A snake, too, was with him, slithering over the body. It didn't pay any mind to Duncan. Rather, its eyes feasted on Zack, and soon, it pounced. Over and again, it coiled and lunged its fangs into him. The sight was far too much for Duncan to bear, and he turned toward the house and fled.

Once inside, he bolted the door and prayed

that whatever was happening was ended. But it wasn't. Without delay, a childish scream ushered in from the hallway.

"Ruth!" Although, he wasn't quite sure it was her. "Patrick!"

Duncan ran to the hallway only to see water spilling out from his cracked bedroom door and the sliver of light revealing that it was not clear. It was red.

Once again, Duncan hesitated, unsure of what to do. But soon, his feet began to walk against the current, and as he neared the door, he edged even more reluctantly.

Then, he opened it.

1974

DUNCAN THREW OPEN the back kitchen door. From the other room, though Mom's back was toward Duncan, he could make out that she was sitting on the couch with her face in her hands.

"I'm home," Duncan called out.

Immediately, Mom turned around to face him. Another face poked around the wall. It was James.

"Is that you, Honey?" she said wearily.

Duncan walked through the shadowed kitchen area and into the lamp-lit living room.

"Oh, Duncan," Mom said, sounding relieved.

"You scared me."

"Where's Dad?" Duncan asked.

She looked at James.

"I drove to the usual spots," James said.

"We don't know where he's at," Mom told him.

"What do you mean?" Duncan said.

"Honey, why don't you get into bed? But be quiet. Nat's already asleep."

"I wanna stay down here."

"Honey, go. I'll be up in a minute to tuck you in."

Duncan gave an incredulous look to James, his leg twitching nervously.

"Duncan, Sweetheart. Go upstairs. Get ready for bed."

His eyes finally broke contact with James', his feet plodding up the steps.

Duncan waited under the covers, watching the clock that ticked continuously on the far wall.

The door opened after a good long while. Mom entered without a word and took a seat on the side of his mattress. She held a blue hymnal in her hand.

"Well," she said, trying to smile, "we'll sing on our own."

"Mom?"

"Yeah?" she answered, her eyes red.

"Where's Dad?"

Mom's eyes shifted to different objects all at once, showing that thoughts were running through her head.

"I'm not sure."

"Is he coming back?"

"Oh," she said instantly, "yes. That I'm sure. Dad'll be back."

"So where'd he go?"

"I thought he was at the church building. But when I didn't find him, I called up James and asked him if he could go searching for him. He couldn't find him, either."

"Is that why he was sitting so close to you?"

"What?" Mom said, a bit confused.

"Do you love him?" Duncan asked.

"Duncan."

"He shouldn't be that close," he added, his brow furrowed, his heart beating fast.

"Oh, Honey. Don't you worry. It's not what it

looks like."

"Are you and Dad going to get a divorce?"

She went silent.

"Is James going to be the new dad now?"

"Duncan," she said gently, though with finality to it. "Of course not. James—he's a family friend. You've known him all your life. He's been at nearly every one of our church gatherings and family get-togethers."

"So?"

Mom's eyes seemed to soften. "Honey, are you wondering if what happened between Zack's parents will happen between Dad and I?"

After a bit of hesitation, Duncan nodded solemnly.

She smiled, making him not feel so afraid. "No, Duncan. That will never happen. I love your father as much today as I did when I first met him —more, really."

"You love Dad more now than on your wedding day?" he asked, surprised.

She nodded quite confidently.

"But Dad didn't drink then, did he? Was he like this then?"

"No," Mom admitted. "His current behavior is more recent."

"How can you love him more with the way he's acting?" Duncan insisted.

"You don't know everything, Honey. Dad—he's been through quite a bit. His own father, your grandpa, wasn't so kind to him. He was sort of like how Dad is now. But he drank a lot more. And he even had Dad drink with him. When he was not much older than you."

"Dad was allowed to drink as a kid?" said Duncan.

"That's not the point, Duncan. He shouldn't have ever been encouraged. And your grandma saw that. She saw how it wasn't good for either of them."

"So what'd she do?"

"They left. For a time."

"Where'd they go?"

"Here."

"Here?"

"You know that Great Uncle Myron was your grandma's brother. So they came here."

"They did?"

"And Dad stayed—guess which room? This one. He never told you that, did he?"

Duncan shook his head.

"Well, he can be pretty private. Especially about his younger years."

"Then how'd you two get married?"

"I said they only left for a *time*. But when they came back, his father had—

Mom paused suddenly. "He was gone. But for good."

"But how'd you two like each other?"

Mom's eyes shifted elsewhere. "Well, let's just save—

The door opened a second time, but with so much force that it jarred the wall.

"What are *yooooouuuu* saying?" slurred an aggravated voice.

They both jolted their heads at the sound. Dad, with his hair mangled and eyes bloodshot, glared at Mom.

"You tell him the truth?" he said. "After twelve years, you decided one night to just go behind my back? You know, it was *you* who wanted it this way. It was *you* who asked *me* to keep shut."

"I didn't tell him anything," Mom said, her voice quivering as though a bit frightened.

Dad inched closer to her. He softened his voice, but its power remained charged. "I heard you. You were talking about us."

"You're drunk," she said with a bite to it. "You don't know what you heard."

"I. Heard. You."

"You misheard me."

Dad turned his attention to Duncan now, though it was apparent he had difficulty finding exactly where his son was—his eyes were not completely able to focus. "You really want to know?"

"Stop," Mom interjected.

"You want to know what you are?" he continued on, his eyes still on me. "A bastard."

"Pat! Stop! I thought you were done with this drinking business. I thought you were done acting this way."

"What way?" he said.

"Like your father."

"I'm nothing like my father!" Dad yelled, some spit flying out as he spoke.

"You're every *bit* of your father!" Mom countered, now matching his aggression.

Dad was so close to them now that all he did was reach out his hand, clench his fist onto Mom's shirt, and pull her up to her feet. "I AM NOTHING LIKE HIM!"

"STOOOOOOP!!" Duncan yelled into the air.

Dad turned his head, his tense face now suddenly relaxed. In an instant, his eyes drooped as if filled with sorrow. His voice, too, was now incredibly weak and timid. "I—I'm sorry, Duncan. I'm drunk."

"I hate you…" Duncan whispered under his breath.

But Dad heard it. He let go of Mom's shirt, who then backed up far enough out of his reach. He stood aright, his whole body facing Duncan, his head sagging, his hands now frozen beside him. "You don't really mean that, do you?"

There was an ugly splinter of silence. Then, locking his eyes on Dad's, Duncan said loud enough to avoid repeating it, "I wish you weren't my father."

Mom now also looked at him with a stunned expression on her face. Both gaped at Duncan, speechless for a good while, until Mom glanced at someone else under the doorframe.

It was Nat, who was in his pajamas, with a blanket tucked securely under his arm—and tears in his eyes.

THE WATER RAN QUIETLY through the forest that day. The leaves, too, which were now starting to turn warm in color, refused to rustle. Even the sound of Duncan's own footsteps was padded by the earthen floor.

The inside of the white-clad church building was not much different. The pews sat in lonesome contemplation despite the light refracting on them. The air, when he had opened the entrance doors, did not whoosh excitedly past.

Though, there was something muffled rising from the far end. The sound was coming from the other side of the office door. So he quickly descended the aisle, around the baptistry, and to the back left corner where the door stood ajar.

"Thank you again," Duncan could hear Dad say as he leaned in. "For everything."

"Pat, I'm sorry," said a low-toned, somewhat sandy voice.

"You don't need to leave. Really," Dad said.

"No, really, I do. People might start talking. You know how that is. I should have made my peace a long time ago."

Duncan, without thought, was now leaning on the door itself. It opened. James was standing in front of Dad's desk, talking to him as he sat there.

"James, let's talk sensibly—

"It's for your own reputation."

Suddenly, the two caught him under the doorframe and halted their conversation immediately.

"Duncan," Dad said, clearly about to shift to a new one. "You can come on in. It's okay."

James turned his eyes from him back to him. "As I was saying. I'll be heading out."

James extended his arm to Dad, waiting for his. They shook hands, and then James turned and strolled past Duncan without a word.

For a moment, Duncan simply stood where he was. Then, noticing Dad beginning to write something on a piece of paper, shuffled toward him.

"Does your mom know you're here?" said Dad, looking up at him.

Duncan shook his head.

"Did you want to sit?"

"What are you writing?" Duncan asked him.

"This? It's my resignation letter."

"What for?"

"Do you know what a resignation letter is?"

Duncan shook his head again.

"It's a letter someone writes when he isn't fit to be in the position he's in anymore."

"You don't want to be a pastor anymore?"

"It's not that I don't *want* to be. It's that I'm not qualified."

"Why not?"

Dad gave him one of those looks as if to help him recall what had happened only the other night.

"Who's going to be in your place?" Duncan said.

"Pastor Dan agreed to come down for a few weeks. Until he figures things out."

"What are *you* going to do, then?"

He sighed, "I've signed myself up for a program. I hope to start this next week."

"For how long?"

"A few months. I'm not sure how long. It depends."

"Where is it?"

Dad didn't respond.

"You can't go away," Duncan said. "Mom even said she wants you here!"

Dad put his hand up. "Your mother already knows. She and I have settled on this."

Duncan's skin changed color, his eyes following suit. "You can't go. We need you here."

"I agree. But I have to go away in order to do that. I know that sounds contrary, but—

"Why do you keep doing it?"

"What?"

"You can stop. It's possible. You did it for a little bit."

"Duncan. Please, I don't know how to say this any better. It's just something I need to do...

Something I've been meaning to do."

"Is it Grandpa?"

"What about him?"

"Is that why you're like this?"

He sighed again. "Look. It's complicated."

"Mom told me Grandpa made you this way."

"I don't know what your mom told you about Grandpa or my situation, but—

"Is it because Zack's gone?"

Dad sat frozen.

"It is because of Zack?" Duncan repeated.

Dad looked at his son and how he stood unflinching in front of him. "I had some trouble in this area when I was a teenager. So my mother made the decision to find me some help. I was able to get cleaned up, and I stayed that way for many years. But when Uncle Myron passed away just a few years ago…It took a toll. I was all by myself, handling things on my own. I didn't feel ready. Then, people started coming to me. Having needs. I went back to the one thing I swore I would never go back to. And this time, your mother helped me get back on track."

Dad stopped abruptly, shooting his eyes over

to the window, his lip shaking. "I couldn't help but feel like what happened to Zack was my fault. And so, again, I crawled back to my own vomit."

Though his countenance remained resolved, tears began to bead down his face.

"I'm so sorry, Duncan. Sorry how all this has affected you. I've sinned. Against the Lord. Against all of you. I've not been the father I set out to be. I don't deserve the title of pastor. And I don't deserve the title of father…Oh God, forgive me!"

Dad turned to Duncan again, though there was shame behind his eyes.

"I'm sorry, too," Duncan said. "I shouldn't have said the things I did."

Dad nodded as though accepting his apology.

His son slowly crept up to his desk as tears continued to trickle down his cheeks. He took his scarred hand and placed it in his. "I forgive you, Dad," Duncan said.

Dad squeezed his hand almost too tightly for him to bear. Eventually, Dad eased his grip, and his tears came to an end after a minute or two.

Dad looked up at Duncan from his desk once more. "You want to play some catch? I can finish this later."

The sullen appearance on Duncan's face quickly rolled over, a smile returning again, this time very widely.

Without any delay, Dad rose from his chair, brought Duncan close to his side, and walked out of the church building together.

The parking lot was empty, except for James' black pickup. As they walked past, Duncan noticed he wasn't inside—not even the rifle that he had once seen propped up against the passenger seat.

The two made their way onto the wooded path that led to the crick. They had sauntered at a reasonably brisk pace. As they crossed the bridge, however, Duncan felt Dad's arm stop him like an airbag.

"What?" Duncan said, not understanding why he stopped so unexpectedly.

Dad peered over Duncan's shoulder with a look of sheer terror on his face. Duncan slowly turned himself around. In the far distance, wading in the crick, stood a beast with thick fur and a short tail. Its eyes were black as coal. It hadn't noticed them. Its muzzle pointed toward the water, bobbing in and out as if it were playing with it or searching for food.

"I need you to climb that tree over there," Dad whispered to him.

As he was saying this, they heard what sounded like a truck sputtering into the church parking lot, soon followed by a harsh rap of the door on metal. Both of them had instinctively looked over toward the direction of the sound, but when they had turned back to keep watch on the bear, it was gone.

"Quickly," Dad said quietly to him, pushing him off the bridge.

They hastened as lightly as possible to the nearest tree they could climb. Dad continued to scan the thicket all around him. "The tree. Hurry!" Dad whispered.

But before they could make a step the next step, a figure emerged from the path.

It was Mr. Burns, and he was not looking too well. His face was pale, with deep, dark bags under his eyes. His hair was greasy and unkempt. Worst of all, there was a rifle in his hand, pointing right at them.

He steadily motioned their way. "I knew I'd find 'ya here!"

"Bill. Put that down," Dad said with his hands up in the air.

"'Ya told us to go away," Mr. Burns said, "just so you could kill him."

"I don't know what you're talking about. But look. We have to get to safety. There's a bear in these woods!"

But Mr. Burns didn't stop. He walked right up to them, just a few feet away, his aim now clearly on Duncan.

Dad tried to step in between them, but Bill yelled out, "Don't move! None a 'ya!"

"Bill. What is this?" Dad said, forced to stand right where he was.

"My kid for yours," Mr. Burns said, refusing to take his eyes off Duncan.

"What for!"

"Like I said. You knew what he'd do—*Aahh*!!" Mr. Burns cried out, his knees bending weakly. A snake had latched onto his calf. He used the butt of the rifle to knock the snake, but not without some flesh taken out first.

"No one killed him, Bill," Dad said, resuming the conversation.

Mr. Burns aimed the rifle back at Duncan. "HE'S DEAD, AIN'T HE?!"

Dad saw the tears welling up in Mr. Burns' eyes, so he said very gently, "Bill. This is a mistake. Let me help you—

"You've done 'nough helpin'! Now it's my turn!"

Duncan saw him switch off the safety lock and just as quickly place his finger on the trigger. Duncan shut his eyes just as a shot was rung through the woods and right past his ear.

Without hesitation, Dad latched onto Mr. Burns' gun. "RUN!" he cried to Duncan. "RUUUN!!!"

Duncan shook off the sudden stupor that chained him to the ground and began sprinting toward the tree. It took all of four seconds before he heard the second shot.

Turning around, Duncan saw his dad stumble backward into the crick.

"DAAAAAAAAAAD!!!"

Mr. Burns heard something rushing quickly toward him, so he turned his gun to the direction of the sound, but the bear that made it was too quick. It pounced on Mr. Burns, who fell backward onto the forest floor. The beast dragged him a few yards into the water before opening its jaws and clamping onto him.

Then, a third shot was heard. Then, a fourth. Then, a fifth. Duncan looked to his left to find James springing up swiftly from the dense vegetation. He moved steadily toward the bear, which had suddenly stopped feasting on Mr. Burns and was now stumbling as if it were dizzy. Duncan saw where it was going to fall. Dad, who was kneeling in the water, clenching both bloodied hands to his red-stained side, was only three yards away. He, too, saw the beast overshadow him. And in a matter of moments, Dad could no longer be seen.

James dropped his rifle, ran into the water, and began using all his strength to move the beast.

"Duncan. Come over here. Help me."

Duncan hurried over to the scene, making sure to look away when passing Mr. Burns, now lifeless in the water.

"Come on. We need to get it off him."

He crouched down next to James and placed his shoulder against the fur.

"One. Two. Three. PUSH!"

And they pushed.

"One. Two. Three. PUUUSSHH!!"

Nothing.

"Get your mother. Quickly."

Mom had her green pastel apron on—a sign that she was in the middle of making supper—when the kitchen door slammed against the counter.

"Duncan, what's the matter?" Mom said, noticing the distraught look on her son's face—not to mention the wet clothes and red marks.

"It's Dad…"

Mom seemed to understand for some reason. "Where is he?"

"By the bridge."

She didn't even bother to take off her apron. "Go. Dial 911." Mom hasted out the door, in which Duncan swore he could hear her crying, "Oh, God, please don't take him! Oh, God!"

His hands shook terribly as he picked up the corded phone on the wall and rang the number. As he did so, he noticed Nat staring apprehensively at him from the table, who had been eating a bowl full of black olives.

"You wait here for them, okay?" Duncan said to him after finishing the call.

Nat watched Duncan dart out onto the backyard again, after Mom. Duncan couldn't recall a time that he had sped faster than that moment. So much anticipation ran through his veins that he was almost hopeful at what he was about to find.

But the truth was, Duncan only heard weeping as he neared the water. Soon, he emerged from the path to see Mom crying in James' arms as they leaned against the beast.

Duncan stopped running when he caught sight of them. The adrenaline now churned into a sour feeling. His feet came to a halt right before the water as if stepping in would bring sudden affliction.

Mom reached her arm out for him. At first, Duncan stayed where he was. But after having taken in the scene for a moment, he waded into the water and joined them. James had his arms over Mom as she coddled Duncan. The sadness that brewed inside bubbled up in a matter of seconds and erupted into silent, painful tears.

1998

THEY WALKED AMONG THE GRAVESTONES, Ruth holding onto one of Duncan's hands with Patrick trailing behind. The cloudless sky created the illusion that it was warmer than it was, so they hadn't worn enough layers to brace the searing wind.

As they walked up the hill, Ruth caught sight of them first. She tugged on Duncan's hand as they made their way over to the stones. The first one they stopped at was his dad's. At the top was etched a simple cross. Below it read:

Patrick Lee McLaughlin
Born February 6, 1941
Died September 20, 1974
Husband & Father

Peering over to his right, Duncan noticed his boy, Patrick, caught by the attention of another stone just a few feet away. Still, he and Ruth remained where they were for another minute more.

Patrick felt a hand gently resting on his shoulder as Duncan walked up behind him. The stone read:

Rachel Jordan McLaughlin
Born June 11, 1960
Died October 22, 1993
Wife & Mother

Ruth squeezed her father's hand tightly, and he brought Patrick into his embrace, who rested his head against his side. Patrick's face was wet, his breathing uneven. They let the wind speak for them. They simply stood and wept and remembered.

PATRICK TOSSED THE BASEBALL underhand to Ruth, who reached out with her mitt to grab it, but it hit the ground before she could react. He jogged over to her and picked up the ball.

"Here," he said. "Like this."

He placed the baseball in Ruth's glove. "Now *you* try."

Duncan sat on the back porch swing, looking out onto the backyard, watching them. Patrick went back over to his spot and threw the ball again. For the second time, it hit the ground before Ruth could open her glove.

"You may want to start a little closer," Duncan called out to them.

Just then, a ring came from the house. At first, Duncan was going to let it sound, but after seeing Ruth miss the baseball for a third time, he thought he'd walk in and pick it up.

"Hello?" he said into the phone.

Duncan. It's Nat.

"Hey, Nat. What's going on?"
It's Mom... You better come home.

THOUGH RUTH WAS IN THE BACKSEAT, she spotted the house right away.

"That's Papa and Nina's house!" she said, pointing with excitement.

They turned, parked, and stumbled out onto the driveway. Patrick stretched as he found his footing on the blacktop. Duncan stopped Ruth as she tried to take their backpacks and duffle bags from the car. Duncan helped her out, and the three went to the front porch.

Nat must have known they had arrived because the door opened right as they approached the landing. He looked at the kids and smiled. Ruth released her dad's hand and rushed to jump into his arms. As Nat was being embraced by both Ruth and Patrick, he gave Duncan a painful look.

"Good to see you, brother," Nat said.

He kissed Duncan as he went through the threshold, where they discovered an array of cardboard boxes scattered across the floor—some empty, some full.

"James and I have been going through the house and packing," Nat told Duncan.

"While Mom's still here?"

"That's what she asked. I think she wants to know we're moving on."

He led them down the hall into what used to be the guest room. The door stood ajar, a faint light emanating into the hallway.

Duncan opened it, and there was Mom lying in bed, who appeared almost thirty years older than she actually was. James, who was reading in the chair beside her, wandered his gaze upward, his reading glasses on.

Duncan shuffled the kids toward Mom, who reached out her thin hand to grab one of theirs.

"Oh, look at you both!" she said happily to the children, though her voice was incredibly weak compared to the last time they had seen her.

Patrick and Ruth went over and gently hugged her as she kissed them on their faces.

James ambled over to Duncan, both of his hands in his pockets. But then he turned and watched Mom talk to the kids.

"Duncan," Mom said.

"Mom."

She looked over to James. "Take the kids, would you?"

He quietly guided them out of the room so that it was just her and her son.

"Come on, now," she said, patting her bedside. "Sit down right here."

So he did.

"You don't need to feel this way," she said, examining his disconsolation.

"…You can't," murmured Duncan.

"What? *Die*? Sweetie, death is one of the only certainties in this life. But our lives don't belong to it anymore. Not one piece."

Duncan's stare slowly drifted downward.

"I'm sorry, Duncan. I know you've missed your father all these years. And I wasn't much help at all."

"It's all right."

"No, Honey. It's not. I shouldn't have tried to stuff him away. I…I missed him, too. But I felt ashamed. I loved your father, but I confess, it was difficult toward the end. When he died, I felt guilty. And so, I did the thing I thought would bring me peace." She smiled regrettably. "But there was no peace. It didn't matter how many things I tried to get rid of. I could never—*would never*—get rid of *you* boys. And you always reminded me of him."

She paused for a moment, trying to find the right words. "Honey—

"I forgive you, Mom. Really."

She looked at Duncan. "There are so many things I wish I could have shared with you. I want you to know that."

"I believe you."

"I never threw anything away. They were always kept in a corner in the attic. They may still be there unless Nat or James did something with them. I want you to have them."

Duncan nodded.

Mom reached her frail hand and softly touched Duncan's face as she would when he was younger. He brought his face low and buried it in her embrace. She held him with all the strength she had left.

*   *   *

A GOOD PART OF THE DAY WAS SPENT sorting through boxes with Nat. From about lunch onward, he and Duncan sorted through paperwork and other files, organizing them in their respective boxes. Eventually, he had to stand up and fix himself something to eat. Ruth and Patrick had been sneaking things from the fridge throughout the day, so he was not so concerned about feeding them.

Duncan put together a meager cold-cut sandwich—a few slices of ham and one piece of provolone. No condiments. White bread. It filled the belly.

As he sat at the kitchen table, Duncan heard someone speaking from the other side of the wall. Looking out the window, he saw James sitting on the back porch with hands clasped together.

"Oh, Father," he heard him pray. "Heal her. But if not, guard the family. Bring comfort to my boys. Give Nat the needed strength. And grant my son, Duncan, peace. Take care of them. Show them Your glory, and remind them each day of

Your steadfast love. Whatever You have for me, I will accept. This life is Yours, not mine. But I also know that what is Yours is now mine also."

Duncan turned away from the window and walked into the living room with the remainder of his sandwich, where Nat was still on the floor, flipping through sheets and sheets of paper.

Duncan sat on the couch. "Where does James sleep at night?" he asked.

Nat stopped and looked at him. "In that chair next to her."

"He sleeps *there*?"

"I told him I could help him move one of our old beds into the room, but that old boy wouldn't bargain with me."

"Where will he be when…the time comes?"

Nat frowned. "Since I'm stationed all over the place, he doesn't like the idea of moving in with me. He said there's an apartment in town. The place where he used to live before he and Mom got married."

Duncan nodded, shifting his eyes onto the kitchen window that led out onto the back porch once more.

*   *   *

DUNCAN'S HANDS WERE PRUNES after having washed most of the dishes. Mom and James never installed a dishwasher, so he spent a good portion of the hour at the kitchen sink. Nat was still in the living room, musing over the boxes.

The sun was hanging low now, causing the sky to become orange in color. The trees were almost as thin as they could be, the leaves having nearly all fallen by now. So, it was easy to spot James strolling on the path that led to the crick. Duncan left the remainder of the dishes in the foamy water.

James was leaning over the railing of the bridge when Duncan caught sight of him. James looked in his direction, not sure who was there at first.

"What are you doing out here?" Duncan said as he sauntered over to him and leaned on the bridge, just as James was doing. "So, anything else you've kept from me?"

"Where is this coming from?" James asked.

"Nat told me you won't sleep in a bed."

"That's not true."

"You're saying Nat lied to me?"

"I've slept in a bed. A few times."

"You're not twenty anymore," Duncan told him. "You can't do this to yourself. You need proper rest."

"If I can be honest, why is my good suddenly so important to you?"

"I just…I can't allow you to let yourself go," Duncan said. "Mom. She's not going to get better. No matter how many times you bring her soup or sit by her bed while she sleeps."

"I know," James said quite casually.

"A day's going to come when she's not going to be there when you go into the room. And what are you going to do then?"

"Duncan—

"I just—I can't let you keep doing this to yourself."

"Duncan. You seem really worried about this."

"She's your wife. Doesn't this situation upset you?"

"No," he answered. "Do you know what grieves me? Knowing that my own father won't be there when I see her again." James stopped leaning on the bridge so he could face Duncan. "You talk as if she'll be gone forever. And there's some truth to that. She won't be here. But what fools are we to have the hope of Christ and let death have the victory? There are people like my father who don't have that hope. I'll cry over them. But I won't cry over your mother."

James put his hands in his pockets like he often did. "I wish things could have been different. Between you and me."

He looked at Duncan for a moment, then started to amble down the bridge.

"And where do you plan to live?" Duncan said, stopping him.

James turned around.

"You can't just go back to your old apartment," Duncan added.

"Then where do you suggest?"

Duncan hesitated, but said, "With us...With me."

James stood utterly still for a moment. Then, he said, "And go back to my old house?"

"Look, James. I want you to move in with my

family. I know I haven't respected you as a father or loved you like a son. But I've come to realize that you watched over him. I know that. And you watched over me, too. I didn't want to see that. But I do now."

Duncan paused to take in the sounds of the running water below. "I've not been the kindest toward you all these years. I know I can't go back and rewrite them."

He looked away from James in fear of showing his face. "If I wasn't so unkind, I could have been with Rachel. In her last moments."

James saw Duncan's shoulders beginning to bob, and he slowly walked back up the bridge. James stood beside him and placed his hand on the back of Duncan's neck. At first, it just stayed there, but after a few moments, he rubbed it gently, just as Dad used to do.

"And I blamed you for my father's death," Duncan confessed.

"Well," James answered, "I blamed myself for a while, too. So I understand. There's always a culprit, so we think. And there is. But I'd say it's rarely the one to whom we point our fingers."

James continued to rub Duncan's neck, as well as his shoulders and back, which he'd never done before. "I know how much you loved him," said James. "Your mother told me that you would see him, as if he's really there…Does that still happen?"

Duncan nodded. "I know it's all inside my head. I know the dead know nothing of the happenings of this world anymore. But in those moments, they feel so real."

"Death. What an enemy. There's something truly demonic going on, far beyond what we think or believe. Or what we merely see. But I thank God you and I now have the upper hand."

He kept his hand on Duncan for a moment more before letting go. "Don't be so doubtful, Duncan," he said as he ambled away. "You *will* see the goodness of the Lord in the land of the living."

"When?" Duncan called out to him, who was now on the path back toward the house.

"When he opens your eyes," James called back while he disappeared into the leafless thicket.

The water engulfed Duncan's sense of hearing as he tried to watch the current below him.

Though, after a while, even the water that trickled along became muffled. What rose in its place were frustrated thoughts, his breathing shortened, his face boiling.

"I thought You had a wonderful plan for the lives of Your people," Duncan said aloud to God. "But they're dead! And I live with such grief. Why have you done this? Tell me—!!

Without warning, the platform underneath him shook dangerously, and the water from the crick writhed until it lashed itself on the side of the bridge. The wind whirled at such incredible speed that Duncan fell over onto his back and was pinned down with its great force.

Then he heard a voice boom out of the whirlwind, like that of thunder.

Dress for action like a man. I will question you, and you will make it known to me. Where were you when I laid the foundations of the earth? Tell me, if you have understanding. Who determined its measurements? Surely you know! Or who stretched the line upon it?

The voice continued, *Have you entered into the springs of the sea, or walked in the recesses of the deep? Have the gates of death been revealed to you, or have you seen the gates of deep darkness? Have you comprehended the expanse of the earth? Declare, if you know all this!*

Trembling seized Duncan's entire body. He could not speak a word.

Shall a faultfinder like yourself contend with the Almighty? The voice echoed. *He who argues with God, let* him *answer it!*

The whirlwind continued to fury. Eventually, Duncan found his voice and yelled back, "Help me, Lord! Help me!!"

Then, just as quickly as it came, the gusty wind ceased, the chaotic waters hushed, and the voice did not rise to speak again. Duncan was alone on the bridge once more, but remained on the ground, trembling still.

"If this is what you have for me," Duncan mumbled through the tears, "help me accept it."

Glancing up, he noticed a snake only two feet away. At first, he rose to his feet, afraid of what would happen. But when he narrowed in on it, its head was completely flattened, as if crushed with immense strength. The rest of the body was strewn lifelessly behind it.

THE SKY WAS A DARK BLUE by the time Duncan found his way back to the house. When he opened the door, the first thing he looked for were the pictures and paintings on the wall. Although, everything seemed perfectly normal—quite unlike the aftermath of an earthquake.

Nat must have decided to continue with the boxes another time, since he was no longer in the living room. The ceiling thumped, signaling that the kids were running around upstairs. And there was James, who had just slipped out of Mom's room and was blowing her a kiss before turning around the corner and out of sight.

Duncan was by himself, though it was too early to check in for the night. So he wandered back into the living room, where he began to clean up the space. His only goal was to shift the boxes to the edges of the room so they could at least meander without feeling like there were tripwires everywhere.

But something stopped him. A pretty large

box surrounded by boxes of smaller sizes and different shapes came into view. On the side of it was written, *James' Photo Albums.*

Out of curiosity, Duncan dismantled the fortress of boxes to reach that particular one. It was heavier than he expected it to be, though he managed to carry it to the couch, where he flicked on a lamp and began to rummage through it. The album cover on the very top read: *Duncan.*

He took the album out of the box, where a cream-colored envelope with his name on it fell from inside it onto his lap. It was the very same one Duncan remembered being given right before his first year of college. Although he had never opened it, it still remained sealed to this day.

For a moment, he wondered if he even wanted to open the album. But interest pushed him, and Duncan began to flip through it.

The very first page was filled with letters. With a closer look, those letters were from his father, written to James. Without taking time to read them, Duncan flipped the page and found baby pictures of himself. One of Mom holding him in the hospital. Another of Dad feeding him. An eclectic array of photos stashed the album in no meticulous order. But as Duncan continued to view the images, he saw James pictured there. One in particular was of him helping Duncan blow out his birthday candles. Duncan was only a toddler.

James cropped up more and more as the album went on as if he held some special place in the family even that long ago. Unable to interpret these sporadic photos, Duncan placed the album under his arm and bounded toward Mom's room.

But when he opened the door, his current thoughts immediately flew away.

"Mom?" Duncan whispered.

But no movement of life stirred within her. She lay with her eyes closed, the blue hymnal open by her side. Cautiously, he went over to it, turning it around to see what she had been singing:

Be still, my soul, the Lord is on thy side
Bear patiently, the cross of grief of pain
Leave to thy God, to order and provide
In every change, He faithful will remain
Be still, my soul, thy best thy heavenly Friend
Through thorny ways, leads to a joyful end.

Duncan sat in the padded chair that James apparently had been sleeping in, took her hand, which was cold, and gently rubbed it with his fingers as though she were still there. He rocked back and forth, humming the tune for her.

James' letter was still clenched in his other hand. At first, he was going to place it on the desk where he had done so with the album. But then, he breathed in deeply, flipping the envelope over and breaking the seal.

1964

DUNCAN,

Today is October 22, 1964. You're three years old. It's your birthday. Your family had a big cake for you. It was carrot cake. While all the other three-year-olds would probably want chocolate, you asked for something with vegetables. So your mama made you that. You liked it a lot. Probably what you didn't realize was that I like carrot cake, too.

We have a lot more in common than you think. As of right now, at least, you are unaware.

That is to be expected at this point. You're young. You have a lot of growing up to do. And so do I. And maybe, Lord willing, when you are older (and both of us are wiser), I may have the courage to share with you what I long to have you know. And I pray earnestly that by that point, you may find it in your heart to forgive me.

Today was the second time I have seen you face-to-face. The first time changed my life forever. But even before I disclose that, you must be told a few things so you can better understand. There is a person I am indebted to, a man whom I look up to and admire. That man is the one whom you call *Dad*. In days of old, even when I was as young as you are, he and I knew each other. We were friends. And your mama—she was part of our lives, too. Your dad lived just across the street from where I grew up. He came over, my father would say, far too often. We'd always find something to do together, even if it was to do nothing.

Now, there came a time when both of us grew older. A time when we began to understand that of promise and loyalty. We made a pact that we would always be there for one another throughout our lives. I must confess, I have not kept my end of the bargain. But it was the promise made those many years ago and persisted by your dad that brought you and I together.

As our childhood reached its high school years, your dad moved away. But before he did, he made another promise. That he and I would both see each other again. And by the hand of God, this came to pass. He and I met again in college. And your mama—she was there, too.

At that time, she and I did not know the Lord. But your dad—during the time he went away—he came to know Him. And so, when we all attempted to reconnect again, things were different. Your dad was different.

Your mama was able to reconnect with him better than I could. They were able to continue on as good friends once again. But it was hard for me. Your dad was not the same person I grew up with. He talked differently. Walked differently. Thought differently. There was a way about him that repulsed me. Needless to say, we drifted apart within our first year of college.

Your mama and I were still close, however. I

would say—knowing what I know now—too close. We were so close that she became pregnant. And, perhaps to your surprise, that little baby in her womb was you.

She had told me two months after she knew. It took her that long to find the words. And it was at this point that I committed the worst sin of my life. It is this moment that I abhor with absolute regret. Upon hearing this news about a baby soon to be born—my child—I decided to enlist myself in the army. And within two weeks, I was packed up and gone.

Your mama was alone, abandoned by the man she thought loved her. She tried to contact me— several times. By phone. By mail. I responded to none of them. I was too preoccupied with forgetting all the missteps that led me to where I ended up.

But your dad, when he saw with his compassionate eyes the shame your mama bore— pregnant, unmarried, and alone—he took her in and made her his own. He loved her in ways that still escape me. What I have come to understand is that he remembered the promise he made to me when we were children. By marrying your mama, he not only loved her, he loved me as well. He took in the fatherless child of his lost friend and covered the humiliation of the woman he disgraced. It was this act of grace that began to open your mama's eyes to the love of Christ. Soon after he married her, she, too, came to know the Lord.

As for me, I was a hopeless wanderer. I will spare you this portion of my life. Though, I find it necessary to share at least this: ready to die, there were many instances in which I tried to kill myself. It was a dark and shadowy season. Take my word for it—there are diabolical spirits that lurk in this world.

Yet, all the while, there is a providence that overrules all the schemes of Satan. I did not come to suspect this until that night when I saw you for the first time. On leave from the army, I made it my mission to never return. There could only be one way out, of course, and I decided a rope would do it.

Your dad, on the other hand, knew I was back somehow. And to my disbelief, he appeared on my front porch, on the street in which we had grown up together, on the very night I had planned to leave this life. Yet he wasn't alone. You were there sleeping in his arms, no more than six months old.

For a moment, I thought the child was his. But then he began to share with me all that had transpired over the course of nearly two years. In all this time, I had not corresponded with your mama. Or with your dad. And so the fact that he stood there on the eve of my supposed end with *my* son arrested me.

He handed you over to me. And when I saw your precious face, all the evil wrought within myself loomed over like a heavy shadow, with all its shame and misery. I could not bear to look at you, the one I had forsaken.

Your dad stood there as I kept you in my arms. All my faculties buckled. I realized that death brought on by my own hand would only be another selfish act on my part. All this time leading up to that night, I convinced myself I would never see you. Yet there you were, breathing gently, your eyes dreaming. It was at that moment that I decided to live.

Since that night, your dad and I kept in touch. Your mama was still hurt by what I had done, so I did not hear from her. But in those following months, your dad—through the form of letters—shared with me of the One who not only gives life, who not only sustains life, but is Himself Life. He told me of Jesus.

I still have that letter your dad wrote about salvation. He brought up Hosea 6. Once he explained it to me, I understood. I understood at least enough to know that I wanted Christ. I longed to be reconciled to Him. How that all of one's trespasses are unmarked when he finds joy in Him. And so it came to pass that very day when my heart was awakened. Awakened for Him. The eyes of my heart had finally seen Him. At that very moment, I was set free. Free from the consequences of my sins. Free from the shame and misery that bound me. Free from the hatred that plagued me. Free to live and to live fully. To live for Christ—my life.

I write these things so you may be encouraged, not that the greatest of men sin, but that even the greatest of sinners repent and are forgiven. And not only forgiven but receive a change of heart. This is true of me, my son. It is only from this side that I finally see clearly. Where I can look on you without deep humiliation and hope that I may be reconciled to you one day— Lord willing, one day soon. Where our eyes will meet and see one another for who we truly are. Not with eyes of bitterness but of tenderness, of compassion, and of love.

It was this hope that spurred me on. But, I must admit that going to war when I knew you were here nearly killed me. Every day, I could not stop thinking of you and how precious you were to me. A new kind of pain entered my heart—the awareness of being isolated from you. Yet, at the same time, I had a sense of motivation to live so I could return. Of course, you did not know of me. I made it very plain to your dad not to say anything.

I'm home again, but not for long. Though, while I have been here, your dad requested that I come over for your birthday. Excitement and fear had been fighting with my heart since the invitation. Through the photographs your dad sent inside each letter, there was an excitement in finally seeing you face-to-face, yet fear of what your mama, whom I had also forsaken, would say.

I came anyway. I stood on your front porch with bated breath and a heart still in battle. Though, in a matter of moments, the door swung open. It was your Great Uncle Myron. I told him who I was, and a moment later, your dad entered the frame. He embraced me and welcomed me inside. Just beyond the foyer, where the kitchen was, stood your mama. She was giving you a snack to tide you over before supper. And when she heard me come in, I saw her glance my way with those methodical eyes. And to my surprise, she smiled—a smile I well remember. It was genuine.

She strolled over to me with you on her hip and, before placing you in my arms, kissed me on the cheek. No words were spoken at that moment, but I understood. She had forgiven me.

We had an early supper—enough time to enjoy much more of the evening sun. I sat under the awning with your mama while gazing out at the crest of the wood where you and your dad were playing cheerfully. It was a needful conversation your mama and I had on that back porch swing. I was relieved to know she had indeed absolved me and was looking forward to having this time to begin making amends. And she made an offer to me, which reminded me of the promises your dad had made and kept. She said she had discussed things with your dad. And they both came to the conclusion that they would keep the origin of your life to themselves until I was ready. That I could be the one to share with you how it all came to pass. They would wait for me. And until then, they offered me great access to you. I could be as much a part of your life as I wanted, she said. What a trembling thought.

I had nothing at that moment to say in return. Just silence. Then, sadness, knowing that in a matter of days, I would be off again. Even now, I'm contemplating how I could be with you. I pray that the Lord be kind to me and hold me fast while we are apart once more.

I will make sure to count my blessings. One of them is the time I spent with you today. At the end of it all, when I thought it was time for me to leave, you strode over and asked that we go on a walk in the woods. You said you wanted to show me something. You took my hand, which was much bigger than yours, and led me to a little crick that winded itself through the trees. You beamed up at me like a man who had shown off his life's work. I couldn't help but laugh. You laughed, too.

I brought you in close as we sat at the water's edge. A deer slowly made its way over to the crick, unassuming, and we watched together as it drank its fill and eventually went another direction. Then, it was just you and me. Your eyes closed, and your breathing grew heavy. I felt the warmth of your skin on mine as I browsed you gently with my finger, hoping not to wake you. And while you dreamt in my arms, I wept.

I will long for this moment—to hold you close once again. I do not know when or how you will come to know the truths divulged here, but I ask that it be received with a heart of mercy. It does grieve me to know that you would come to find that your own father had abandoned you. This haunts me every day.

Despite this, however, it is my sincere hope

that in the following years, I will find the courage to confess the truth to you. But if it were the Lord's will that you come to find the truth later on, I ask that you may not think less of me for withholding these things. I am not a perfect man. Far from it. I still have sin wrought in me, and I am still learning right from wrong despite the fact that I have been redeemed by Christ—not to mention I am much older than you.

Above all, do not despise Him who has been so kind to you—to us both. This life—it's fleeting. What a waste it would be to reject the One who has loved you so sweetly. Even more than wanting you to grasp the truth that I hold, it is the life-giving truth that is held by the Father, which I yearn for you to obtain. All you need to be is silent. Listen. You'll begin to hear His gentle voice. See the works of His hands. And maybe, by His loving grace, you'd realize Him standing among you, reaching out, welcoming you into the Kingdom.

I love you, my son. Forevermore.

1998

THE SNOW FELL QUITE HARD over the past several days. If it weren't for the plow truck that finally came down their road early in the day, no one would have been able to tell where the blacktop ended and the yard began. Though, Patrick and Ruth were happy. They were hoping for a white Christmas.

It was already dark, except for the houses that lit up the street with their decorations. The home Duncan approached, however, was shadowed by its non-celebration. The only way he knew there was someone inside was due to a faint, warm light shining through the window.

He knocked on the door with a small wrapped gift in hand. No one answered, so he tried again, leaning his ear against the door to hear if someone was coming.

Nothing.

Duncan sighed, resigning to place the gift on the doorstep, hoping the next bit of snowfall wouldn't completely cover it.

It wasn't until he walked over to his own yard and fully stepped inside his home that the door finally opened. The old man looked down to find a present at his feet. He bent down, picked it up, and examined it in one of his hands. Scanning around to ensure Duncan was not hiding somewhere—he decided to open it.

The gift was about the size of a small jewelry box. In fact, that was what it was wrapped in. The old man opened the black case to find one, small, colorless photograph. It was of him when he was a younger man. And his ten-year-old son was in there, too, standing in front of him.

He flipped the photo around to find it written in calligraphy: *Hosea 6:1.*

The old man stole one more glance toward Duncan's house across the street before scurrying back inside and shutting his door reluctantly.

Meanwhile, Duncan opened his own front door to find Ruth on Patrick's shoulders, attempting to put the star on the top of the tree.

"Need some help with that?" Duncan said, rushing over to meet them.

"I got it, I got it!" Ruth said, refusing his hand.

Nat and his wife emerged from the kitchen with plates and silverware.

"We're about ready," James said, appearing also from the other room, wearing Mom's old apron.

"Is Grandpa Tom coming?" Patrick asked as he placed Ruth down from his shoulders.

Duncan shook his head.

"It's all right," Nat said. "We'll try again tomorrow. It's only Christmas Eve."

"Come on, Daddy!" Ruth said, taking her father's hand. "I'm hungry!"

Nine plates were set at the dining table, although only six of them were sitting there. Ruth

227

immediately reached for a roll the moment she situated herself on a few pillows.

"Not yet," Patrick whispered to her.

James stretched out his hands, and everyone did the same, locking them with each other's. They all bowed their heads.

"God our Father," James prayed, "Almighty and True. Thank you for Your blessed Son, who was brought forth in the flesh to be with us, whom we celebrate today. And every day. Thank you for all You've done through Him and…"

James' prayer seemed to quiet to a distant, indistinguishable hum as Duncan opened his eyes. There, on the other end where the three extra plates brandished the table, sat three people he knew very well. Rachel on one side. Mom on the other. And Dad, who was in the middle. All three of them looked back at Duncan, smiling.

"…We pray this all," James' prayer rose to Duncan's attention again, "in Your holy Son's name, Christ Jesus. Amen."

"Amen," everyone said in response.

A moment later, the chatter resumed in full strength, and Duncan realized that those three chairs in which Rachel, Mom, and Dad were sitting were now empty, as they had been the whole time. But Duncan realized something else —a family was still with him, and they were smiling, too.

DUNCAN COLLECTED THE REMAINING three plates later that evening, handing them to James, who placed them back in the cupboard.

"Come on, Dad!" Patrick yelled from the living room, sitting beside the tree where there were wrapped boxes laying everywhere.

"We're opening presents already, are we?" James laughed.

Ruth pulled on James' arm, and he let her escort him to a chair near the tree. Nat and his wife sat on the couch together, drinking the last bit of their decaf coffee. But Duncan stood under the frame that led into the dining room, watching them from afar.

Everyone began to open their gifts excitedly, but Duncan was only watching one of them. James, who was handed a present by one of the kids, began unwrapping it carefully. Once he knew what it was, he hurriedly ripped the remainder off.

It was the photo album that Duncan had discovered just a month prior. James opened it to find that old cream-colored envelope addressed to Duncan, its seal broken, the letter no longer inside.

Immediately, James turned his face to Duncan, his casual expression now switched to deep surprise. There was a smile on Duncan's face as he leaned against the frame, along with a deep-seated peace.

Yes, Duncan was sure—the eyes of his heart had finally seen him.

Come, let us return to the Lord;
For he has torn us, that he may heal us;
He has struck us down, and he will bind us up.

Hosea 6:1

THANK YOU

As a small, independent author such as myself, I am incredibly grateful that you have taken the time to journey through these pages. What probably had taken you a few short hours to read has been eight years worth of writing, revisions, and rewrites.

If this story has affected you in some positive way, would you be willing leaving a rating or review on the site in which you've purchased this book? Doing so will help others feel confident to pick up this story, and it will help spread a message we all desperately need to hear.

Please feel free to share this story with friends, families, coworkers, classrooms, and loved ones.

SPECIAL REGARDS

THERE ARE SO MANY whom I am indebted to, the first and foremost being Christ. Had He not shown me such a wonderful salvation back in 2011, I would not have been able to write about His magnificent, magnanimous love.

To my parents, Myron and Tamara, who showed their unrelenting love by adopting my brother, Nathan, and myself in 1999.

To my twin brother, Nathan, whom I have had the privilege of growing to care for and appreciate over these 26 years.

To my other brothers and sisters whom I have gathered throughout my life, whom I love dearly, and whom I cherish as my very own.

To Paul (Jay) Yasnowksi, whom I have been able to witness such a wondrous change of heart, and whom I am able to call my eternal brother.

To those in my local church, Grace Reformed Baptist Church, who epitomize grace and patience—especially toward me.

To my beta readers who, to my benefit, did not spare an opinion: Lee Bratton, Wade and Peggy Coley, Jonathan Goodwin, Dr. Rosalie de Rosset, Julie Way, James Williams, Dan Woolley.

To Lisa Hladio, who not only read my final draft, but who spent her free hours reading my 150,000-word original and provided extensive feedback on each chapter.

To so many I am unable to name for one reason or another—you live in my heart.

ABOUT *the* AUTHOR

A.T. LISCHAK was born and orphaned in L'viv, Ukraine in 1998. He and his twin brother were adopted one year later by American parents. Lischak grew up in the small town of Brookfield, Ohio until he went to college at Moody Bible Institute in Chicago. There, he received a bachelors degree in Pastoral Studies in 2021. After an eight-month gap season in New Hampshire, he moved to Owensboro, Kentucky, where he currently lives. He is a member of Grace Reformed Baptist Church.

Lischak began writing this story in 2016 at the age of seventeen.